The Pilgrim

Children of His Promise

Book 1

By

Ronna M. Bacon

Hebrews 11:13

All these died in faith, without receiving the promises, but having seen them and having welcomed them from a distance, and having confessed that they were strangers and exiles on the earth.

Dedicated to my parents, who equipped me to face the storms of life and to understand that I am pilgrim on earth.

Table of Contents

Chapter 1

Chapter 2

Chapter 3

Chapter 4

Chapter 5

Chapter 6

Chapter 7

Chapter 8

Chapter 9

Chapter 10

Chapter 11

Chapter 12

Chapter 13

Chapter 14

Chapter 15

Chapter 16

Chapter 17

Chapter 18

Chapter 19

Chapter 20

Chapter 21

Chapter 22

Chapter 23

Chapter 24

Dear Readers

Chapter 1

Holding his head in his hands, pain throbbing through his whole body, Lincoln Carmichael stumbled through town, garnering looks of disdain, horror and shock. He had no idea where he was, nor did he really care at that moment. His path took him outside of town, towards a lake, he thought. He paused, tilting his head back at the hot sun, his eyes sliding closed as he did that, swaying on his feet. He blinked, his vision blurring, not able to see where he was headed, but he kept putting one foot ahead of the other, moving forward slowly, inch by inch. Finally, he could go no further. He slumped to the porch floor of a cabin, cottage, he wasn't quite sure what it was, and lay still, his body betraying his will to continue. He rolled to his side, his eyes closing, a hand reaching for the door before he lay still. The insects and birds he had disturbed considered him, thought him not a threat, and began their choruses again.

Driving up to her home late that afternoon, Holly Gardiner acknowledged to herself that she was tired. Working long hours in the summer as a landscape artist was fatiguing but rewarding. Still, she felt bereft, as if there was more to life, something she hadn't yet found. She refused to acknowledge to herself that she was looking for a soul mate, a man to share her life with. That she had decided years ago wasn't for her. God hadn't brought anyone into her life, not in this town anyway.

She stood for a moment, her hand on her closed car door, looking around, sensing something was off but not seeing anything overt. She shrugged, heading for the back of her house and into the sunroom. She paused, a frown on her face, once more thinking something was off but not knowing exactly what.

She changed quickly, knowing she had her own gardens to look after, and heading for the front door, pulled her mahogany curls up into a clip. She paused, her hand on the door, sensing that when she opened it, her life was about to change. That scared her. She shuddered as she felt a sense of fear and terror run through her. Lord, I have no idea what is going on. You do. Please, dear Lord, protect me.

Opening the door, she stopped short, her mouth dropping open even as her hand was raised to cover it, her other hand still on the door knob. She stepped back, shutting the door firmly, a hand on it. She shook her head. No, she was seeing things. There was not a battered and bruised man laying on her front porch. She had been reading too many suspense novels, she thought. They were not only playing out in her dreams, now they were invading her waking life.

She cracked open the door again, peeking around the edge, and sighed. She hadn't seen things. There really was a man laying there, not moving. She shoved the door open and tentatively stepped towards him, stopping well back and calling softly for him to wake up and move on.

"Well, Lord. That didn't work, now did it?" She spoke out loud. "Now what?"

She approached closer, her bare toe going out to poke at the man's back, again with no response. "Is he dead, Lord? Heaven help me if he is. I don't need this. I am already in trouble with the police over Jake. Now what?" She turned to search for her collie, Jake, not seeing him. "Hiding are we, Jake? Or are you up to no good again?"

She finally bent over the man, a hand reaching for his neck. "Well, he's alive. That's good, I think. Now what?"

She knelt, her hands reaching to roll him to his back, hearing the groans of pain as she did so. "Now, just what did you go and do? You've been beaten by the looks or it, or been in an accident or something, now haven't you?" Her eyes raised, she searched the surrounding lawn and laneway. "No vehicle. So you've walked here?" She sat back on her heels. "You're the one, aren't you? Ted mentioned seeing someone staggering through town that looked hurt. And somehow you've ended up here."

She stood, her eyes on his face in contemplation, knowing she just couldn't walk away. "I need to get you help, mister, but who do I call?" She finally reached for her phone. Ted would help, she knew. The teenager, almost a man, did odd jobs around town and had become a good friend of hers. She knew his parents quite well. His father was the town doctor, his mother the librarian.

Ted stood for a moment twenty minutes later, staring at the man and then at Holly. "Miss Holly? Where did you get him from?" Shock stood on his face.

Holly bit back a grin, knowing that Ted could and would keep a confidence. "I didn't. He found me, by the looks of it. I need to get him up and out of here."

"There's no way you can take him back to town. I heard someone came through this afternoon, looking for him. Something about a murder."

Holly stared at him, then shrugged. "Then, I guess it will have to be the spare room for now. Come on, then. Let's get him up. Then you can go find your Dad and bring him out here. He needs to assess him."

Ted was away on a run after helping lift the unconscious man into Holly's house and into the spare room. She had thrown back the covers for Ted, and now stood, her eyes thoughtful, before she headed for her office and her camera. She would take pictures of him, she thought, and then sighed. She had to call Dougal, the officer on duty. Village that it was, it wouldn't be long before word got out that she was sheltering the stranger.

She spun as she heard a noise at her front porch and ran to peek out. No, she didn't know that man. Who was it? She turned to glance back at the bedroom and then back to the window, watching as the man searched and then just stood, eyes on the house, before he walked back into the surrounding bush.

"Just what have I gotten myself into, Lord?" She breathed out a quick prayer for safety, before stepping out onto the porch. A paper lay there, where the man laid, one that hadn't been there before.

She reached for it, fear gathering in her heart as she read the threatening words. How had he been found so quickly? And just what was going on with him? Why threaten her?

Chapter 2

Doc stood by the bedside of the man, stethoscope draped around his neck, his eyes thoughtful as he watched Holly carefully washing off the man's face at his request. He shook his head. Now what had she gotten herself into? She had lived in the village of Cairn for all her life, as had he, and she was known for taking in stray animals and helping anyone who needed her aid, often to her own detriment. She just doesn't think about herself, now does she, Lord? Maybe she has something there.

Holly sat back on the edge of the bed, her eyes first on the man, then on Doc.

"Doc? What happened to him?"

"I don't rightly know but I would hazard a guess that he was beaten. It doesn't appear to have been from an accident. You found a wallet on him, you said?"

She nodded and rose, heading for the dresser. She turned, a worn brown leather wallet in her hand. "Here. I send Ted for Dougal."

Doc nodded as he watched her, catching a look in her dark brown eyes that stopped him. Lord, what have You gone and done? Sent someone for Holly to love? He opened the wallet, knowing that he would need to be very careful. Before he could look through it, he heard his son calling for Holly and then Dougal's voice.

Dougal Hunter stood staring at Holly as she explained what she had found and then reached for the note. "This was left? Just random like? Holly, what did you go and do this time?"

Defensive, she crossed her arms and glared at Dougal. "This time? What are you talking about? I never deliberately do things. You know that, Dougal. We've been friends all our lives."

He sighed, running a hand through his dirty blond hair. "I know, Holly. I know. It's just you're always rescuing some critter."

"This is no mere critter." Holly tamped down her anger, and yes, her fright. "This is a man. Doc has his wallet. We need to find his family and let them know he's here. Then they can come get him and take him home." But in the secret portion of her heart that she never unlocked or rather hadn't unlocked for years she wished it wasn't so, that he wouldn't leave her.

Dougal took the wallet Doc handed him and then stood, his eyes on Lincoln's face as he began to toss and turn, pain etched deep. Holly sat once more beside him, her hand reaching for his, her very touch calming him. Dougal frowned and then began muttering to himself. Holly, you've gone and done it now, haven't you? Like I said, this is no stray critter. He's a family somewhere that's likely looking for him. You can't keep him.

Dougal searched through the wallet, pulling out Lincoln's identification and making notes. "He's from Hope, Holly. So how did he end up here in Cairn? That's what, hundreds of miles from here?"

She nodded. "About a hundred, I would say. Dougal?" She turned to face him. "What are you thinking?"

He shrugged, not willing to comment just at the moment. "Can't rightly say yet, Holly. I'll need to contact someone there. Says his name is Lincoln Carmichael. I don't see anything about next of kin in here to notify. Usually people will have that." He looked around and then walked to the dresser where Lincoln's pocket contents had been laid. "No phone?"

Holly shook her head. "I didn't see one. Ted looked around outside and then tried to track back the path this man took. No luck." She turned back to Lincoln, brushing back the deep red hair from his brow, her touch rousing him.

Lincoln's deep gray eyes flickered open and he looked around, his tongue coming out to lick at his dry lips. Doc reached to help him sip at the glass of water he held to his mouth, then stood back, watching carefully as Lincoln searched their faces, his gaze settling on Holly, a plea for help in his eyes.

"Please?"

"Please what?" Holly frowned, not quite sure what was up.

"Don't call my family. Don't call my brother and sister. They're in danger. He threatened them." Lincoln laid his head back, the headache pounding at his temples and driving all coherent thought from him.

"Your family? We need to call them. They need to come and get you. I can't keep you here." Holly was beginning to panic, suddenly realizing just what she had walked into, or so she thought.

Lincoln's eyes opened slowly and he shook his head, pausing at the pain. "No. Don't. Don't call them. He said he'd kill them." His hands shoved at the blankets. "I need to get up. I can't stay here. He's following me. He said I had to do something but I can't remember what it was. I told him no. Please? Help me up." His voice died away as consciousness fled, leaving him laying helpless once more.

Dougal stared at him, then watched Holly closely, before sighing. He knew exactly what she would say. That they had to respect his wishes.

"Don't, Holly." Doc's soft words of warning caught her ear, and she spun to stand in front of him.

"Don't what? Doc? Dougal? We can't just dump him out on the street, or rather out in the woods. You know that. We have to take care of him." They could see the compassion in her bearing and her eyes.

"We have to wait for him to wake up again and tell us why he doesn't want us to call his family."

"Holly, that's exactly what we can't do. We need to call them."

"And tell them what? That he doesn't want them around him? That he's afraid for them? Without knowing why, how can we even explain what he's said?" Holly's defiant stance had her earning smiles from the two men and a silent victory shake of his hands from Ted.

"We'll wait, Holly, only for a couple of days. If he doesn't come around, we will have to call them."

She shook her head. "No, Dougal. We can't. Not until he can explain what is going on." She turned to study the man. "Doc? I gather you'll have Eveline come out as well?"

"She's been away for the day. If you can manage tonight, she'll be here in the morning. At least it's Saturday tomorrow. You don't have to work, do you?" When she shook her head, he continued. "You will sleep tomorrow, Holly. Otherwise, we move him from here tonight. Ted will stay, just to help."

Ted moved to stand beside Holly, shoulders back, standing straighter than his father had seen him. Doc smiled at his son, seeing how his words had spoken to his son, of the trust he had shown him as he treated him as a fully grown man. "Come get me if you need anything, Ted."

Dougal laid the wallet back on the dresser. "I don't like this, Holly. We don't know anything about him."

"I am sure you'll research him or whatever it is you do before the night is over." She hadn't taken her eyes from him. "God brought him here. He will protect us."

Chapter 3

Four days later, Holly paced her living room, her eyes straying every once in a while to the closed bedroom door. Doc had appeared, told her to leave, that he needed to assess his patient. She had reluctantly left and headed for her kitchen, knowing Doc would want tea before he left. She had turned before she reached the room, her hand to her mouth. What if he was worse? What if the man called Lincoln died in her home? She couldn't stay here if he did, and that would break her heart, leaving the home her mother had left to her.

Once alone with Lincoln, Doc quickly assessed him, finding no broken bones as he had feared, but Lincoln was certainly tender over the ribs and kidneys. Doc frowned. He really needed to take Lincoln in for imaging. He just didn't see how he could do that without the whole town knowing, but from the few comments he had heard, the village was aware of just where Lincoln was, but would do everything in their power to protect Holly. He glanced at the door, also knowing he would have a fight on his hands with Holly if he even suggested that very move of taking the younger man to town. He sighed, his eyes on his patient, watching as Lincoln's head tossed from side to side. If we can avoid a fever, we'll be lucky, won't we, Lord? And that's exactly what I think we'll be fighting soon.

Lincoln's movements stopped and his breathing evened out once more. Doc sighed with relief. Missed that one, didn't we? Now to get him healed. Dougal had found him the day before, with a report that he had spoken with someone named Gerry in Hope, who could give no information as to why Lincoln would be on the run. Gerry had been concerned, wanting to come and find Lincoln, or at least let his siblings know. Dougal mentioned in passing that Gerry would keep his confidence but would also be investigating.

Doc turned once more to watch Lincoln, seeing his eyes opening. Doc stooped to assess him, seeing he was alert.

"How are you feeling, young man?"

Doc's voice startled Lincoln, causing him to jerk and turn towards the older man.

"I'm sorry. Do I know you?" His voice was rough and hoarse from disuse.

Doc grinned. "No, I don't think you do. I'm Doc, the local physician. Holly called me to come look at you."

"Holly?" Lincoln twisted his head, searching the room, blinking against the pain. "Where am I?"

"You don't know?" At the negative movement of the head, Doc shook his own. "You are in the village of Cairn, staying with Holly. Do you know her by chance?"

"No, I don't think I do. I'm....." Lincoln's voice died away, and panic began to set in. "I don't know who I am. Who am I?"

"You don't know who you are?" Doc frowned, knowing that there had been a head injury at some point. "You really don't remember?"

"No." Lincoln could feel panic starting to rise once more and he wished for whoever it had been that had calmed him during the nights to return. He needed to feel the touch of that hand on his face, soothing him back to sleep.

Doc shook his head, then moved to call for Holly, who flew into the room, fear on her face. She stopped as she saw Lincoln awake before she moved to kneel by the bedside, her hand going out automatically to touch his face. Lincoln turned to her, leaning against her hand, finding the comfort he needed.

"Doc?" Holly's soft voice caught Lincoln's attention, and he watched intently as she turned to look up at the older man.

"Holly, yes, he's awake and alert. There's only one thing. He can't remember his name."

"He can't?" Holly's eyes turned back to Lincoln, searching his face. "Well, that's not good, is it? How do we get him to remember?"

Doc snorted as her plain statement. That was just so Holly, he thought. "We need to get him healed first, Holly, and then we see. Once he's well enough, we will need to move him to somewhere else. You can't keep him."

Lincoln frowned at the conversation going on around him. Just who where these people, and why would the woman want to keep him?

Holly shook her head at Doc. "I know that, Doc. It's obvious that I can't. Even though he seems to be a stray." She looked back at Lincoln, her other hand going out to grasp his, stopping his fingers as they picked at the blanket. "Your wallet says you are Lincoln Carmichael and that you are from Hope. You are miles from home."

"I'm sorry. I have no idea where that is." Lincoln licked at his lips, trying to moisten them, grateful for the cup of water Doc held to his mouth. "Where am I?"

"In Cairn. Well, outside, sort of. You're a guest in my home." She glared at Doc as he choked back laughter. "Doc, behave yourself."

"I'm sorry, Holly. You just sounded so definite there in your description of where he is." Full blown laughter came from Doc and Holly finally had to smile.

Her smile caught Lincoln's eyes and he stared at her, sure he had never seen a more beautiful woman in his life. Then he sighed. How would he even know? He couldn't even remember his own name, now could he?

"I have family?"

"You do. You mentioned them. Just not who." She paused, her eyes searching his face before she looked up at Doc, who nodded, a grim look on his face. "Lincoln, you need to rest but you really do need to try and remember. You told us someone was after you, that he wanted you to do something and you refused. We need to know who. We can't protect you if we don't know who."

He stared at her for a full moment before shifting his gaze to the physician, meeting his steadfast look. "I....He's....They're......". He finally sighed. "I'm sorry. I just can't remember. Why?"

"You likely had have a brain injury. We need to get you into town for some imaging, but I'm not sure about moving you." He shared a look with Holly, who nodded. "I'll be back later, Holly. We'll see how he is late this afternoon and maybe go from there." Doc stood for a moment, his eyes on Lincoln, who had drifted back to sleep. "He's sleeping now. Let him sleep, Holly. Come, we need to talk."

Holly rose, reluctant to walk away from Lincoln but knowing she had to.

"Doc? What's wrong with him?"

"Amnesia." He paced, his hands in his pockets. "I really need to do that imaging, Holly."

"I know, Doc. But how do we get him there?"

"If you're worried about the village, they know about him, but won't say a word. They are also aware that he is on the run. They will do everything they can to protect you and protect him. You know that." He finally walked towards the door. "I'll see you later. Eveline won't be out today, she needs the day."

"If he's better, then we don't likely need her."

Doc spun. "You do, Holly. You'll overstretch yourself otherwise. I know you."

Holly stood on the porch, watching the dust settle back down, before she rubbed at her arms. Something seemed off today, but she just wasn't sure what. She stepped off the porch and walked around her home, seeking for what she wasn't quite sure. She paused as she saw the footprints in the garden, fear suddenly running through her. Was Lincoln being tracked? Had they found him? She spun, her eyes searching the trees around her home. She should feel safe, here in her sanctuary. She usually did. Today, she didn't. And she didn't quite know why.

She ran for the door, slamming it shut and locking it, before standing her back to it, hand to her throat, willing her thudding heart to slow down. She finally moved away from the door, to stand staring at Lincoln as he slept and then on to the kitchen, where she withdrew the container of broth and moved to heat some. He would need some soon, she knew.

The late afternoon sun beamed its rays through the partly closed curtains and tickled at Lincoln's face as he moved restlessly. His eyes opened and he glanced around, his head feeling clearer but just as thick. He snorted. That really makes a lot of sense, now doesn't it, he thought. He rolled to his side, groaning with the pain as he hit his ribs against the mattress. I hope the other fellow is just as sore as I am. He raised up on an elbow, searching the room, not recognizing it, before he swung his feet to the wooden floor, feeling the softness of well-worn planking under them. He sat for a few moments before he stood, waiting as his head cleared and he could move freely. Well, as freely as the pain let him, he thought. He reached for his shirt, staring at it, not sure if it was even his, but it had to be, since it was on the chair beside him. He pulled on his jeans and then the shirt, his hand feeling along the shirt fabric, a soft flannel, before he turned.

Moving quietly, he searched the room, for what he wasn't even sure. He stopped at the dresser, a hand reaching out to tentatively touch the worn wallet, before he flipped it open and slid out the license, seeing his own face staring back at him. He didn't recognize anything else as he searched the wallet, not finding anything that would help him. That seemed strange, he thought. Don't I have any pictures of anyone with me?

He turned for the door, pausing with his hand on the knob, knowing that when he opened it, his world would change. He bowed his head, confident that he believed in God, and that was the only thing that would get him through what was coming up. Lord, I have no idea where I am, or even for that matter who I am. I need You, like I've never needed You before. He turned the knob, quietly pulling the door open, padding into the other room on his bare feet. He paused, hearing soft singing from the back of the house and headed that way, pausing once more in the kitchen, the aroma of soup and fresh baked bread lingering, causing his stomach to rumble.

He shook his head. No, he wasn't dreaming. Not any more, at least, he hoped. He reached for the back door, pulling it open and then closed behind him, feeling the soft warm breeze on his face as he stood, eyes closed for a moment, and then opening them, looking around. He stepped from the porch, following the sounds of the music, to find Holly kneeling at a flower bed, a large sable collie at her side. The collie stared at him, then rose, heading his way. Lincoln froze, letting the collie sniff at his hand before it nudged under it for petting.

Holly felt Jake rise from beside her and half turned on her knees, surprised to see Lincoln standing in her back yard. What is he doing up? Lord, help me. I just can't do this. She rose, her eyes intent on the man as he rubbed Jake's head, Jake leaning against him as hard as he could, still gentle enough that he didn't knock Lincoln over.

Holly stopped, staring with a frown at Lincoln's bare feet before her eyes raised to his face, seeing him standing with his eyes closed, face raised to the sun for a moment before his head lowered and he stared at her.

"Holly? That is your name?" Lincoln's voice was still rough from disuse and he had to clear his throat to get the words out.

"Holly Gardiner, to be exact. And that is Jake." She nodded towards the house. "You should not be up, you know that."

He shrugged, a small grin on his face. "I couldn't stay in bed any longer. Really. My head does feel better."

She snorted at that. "I'm sure it does, but walking around when you've just gotten up, I don't know about that." She reached for his arm, linking hers through his, and drew him to a bench, shoving against him lightly to make his sit.

Lincoln dropped down suddenly, the jar echoing through his head, causing him to squeeze his eyes shut. When he opened them, Holly stood in front of him, hands to her mouth, her face a picture of shock.

"I'm sorry. I didn't mean to do that. Are you okay?"

He reached for her hand, drawing her down beside him, his eyes intent on the work worn hand he held, covered in dust and dirt and debris from her garden. "I am. Are you?"

She finally nodded, withdrawing her hand from his and reaching for Jake. "I am. How is your head?"

He shrugged. "Okay. But why am I here? Do you know?"

She shrugged and then shook her head. "You really don't remember, do you? I found you on my front porch, unconscious a few days ago. Doc's son helped me move you to my spare room. You've been here since." She sighed, trouble on her brow. "You said someone was after you, that they wanted you to do something. Only you can't remember."

He frowned, his eyes on her face and thought through her words. "I'm sorry. I really don't remember. That's not good. How can I protect you if I don't know who from?"

"Protect me?" Her voice rose to a small squeal. "Who said I needed protection? It's you most likely that does."

He shook his head. "I don't think so. For some reason, and I really wish I could remember why, now that you've become involved in my life, you're in danger too. Something there in the back of my mind."

"And on the tip of your tongue, only you can't find the words to express it." She grinned as he stared at her. "I hate that. It happens to me all the time." She looked at her watch. "I have soup and bread ready for you. Stay here."

He shook his head. "I will not. I am not an invalid, even if you think I am. Let me help you."

She studied him for a moment before she shrugged. "Whatever. If you end up flat on your back again, don't blame me." She rose and strode away from him, leaving him staring after her before he looked down at Jake, whose chin rested on his knee.

"Is she always like that, boy?" His head raised as he heard a noise from the woods and a growl from Jake, who took off after the sound. Lincoln stood, knowing he needed to follow Jake, but also knowing he didn't have the strength or stamina that was required. He sighed. That fellow, Lord? Is he here? Did he follow me? Have I now put Holly and this place at risk from someone I can't even identify?

Chapter 4

A month later, Doc watched as Lincoln paced his office, knowing that the younger man was restless but reluctant to leave Cairn. What do we do with him, Lord? He's moved into our basement apartment, and we are glad to have him here. Holly seems different, more settled but still our outspoken friend, causing mirth to follow wherever she goes.

"Lincoln?" When he didn't respond, Doc rose and went towards him, a hand on his shoulder stopping his movements. "What are you thinking? Are you planning on returning to Hope?"

Lincoln stood, his eyes on the window, watching as the curtains moved slightly at the breeze coming through the screen. He shrugged. "I don't think so. I don't want to endanger anyone else. But I am not sure I should be staying here. Does that make sense?" He turned to watch Doc, knowing that this friend he now had would be honest with him.

"Sit, son.   We need to think this through. But first, we need to pray. I have been and I know you have been as well." Doc finally raised his head, after petitioning for wisdom and clarity. "What do you want to do?"

Lincoln hesitated, knowing that his words might not be taken in the right way. "Holly? Is she really all alone?"

Doc nodded, hope in his heart that maybe, just maybe, God had sent that special person for a friend who gave and gave and took nothing for herself. "She is. Her father disappeared under suspicious circumstances when she was little. We have tried tracing him, but to no avail.   Her mother had always had a heart condition and that took her when Holly had just turned eighteen. It broke Holly. She went away to college, returned here and set up a business for herself. She's done well, able to support herself."   He suddenly grinned.   "She's become known as the "stray lady"."

Lincoln choked on his mouthful of water. "What did you say?"

Doc began to laugh. "She's known in the area as someone who takes in strays and then finds homes for them." Doc pointed at him. "She wanted to keep you."

Lincoln stared at him and then began to laugh. "So that's what you meant, when you said she couldn't keep me?"

Doc nodded. "She would have, you know. Now, what are you planning on doing?"

Lincoln shrugged. "I have no idea. I don't know what I used to do." He watched as Doc looked down. "But somehow, I think you do."

Doc nodded. "Dougal spoke with someone in your home town, a man by the name of Gerry, with the police there. He said you were a lawyer, but that lately you had taken time off from that. He wasn't sure why or what you were planning."

Lincoln sat back, a memory tickling at his mind. "That could be. I just wish I could remember."

"Let your mind heal. It will take time. Somewhere, something or someone will give a hint and you will remember."

Lincoln studied his hands. "I just wish it was different."

Doc reached to lay a hand on the younger man's shoulder. "I know. You want to get to know Holly better and are afraid you have someone in your past. You don't. Dougal was specific when he asked that. You didn't date, we know that. Gerry seemed to think you didn't have time, that your law practice had been too busy."

Lincoln shrugged. "I really don't remember. I just wish I could."

Doc sat back, assessing the man in front of him, finally speaking. "We have no idea who is after you or why, but I suspect it was something to do with your law practice. What that was, only you know."

Lincoln nodded. "I suppose I should go back and go through my office." He was reluctant to do that. He had begun to enjoy life in the village of Cairn and in particular, Holly's company.

"Why don't you sign off on authorization and have Gerry go through your office, seeing what he can find out? That's one step you could take."

He nodded. "I could, but I really don't want to at this point. Can we leave it for now?"

Doc shrugged. "It is your life, but just don't hurt Holly. The village will chase you away if you do."

Lincoln laughed. "They would at that. I feel like I have come home, coming here, even under the circumstances." He rose, pacing the office, finally standing in front of an enlarged photo, peering at the artist's. "This is mine."

Doc rose, coming to stand beside him. "Is it?" He peered at the signature. "I never knew that. You're good."

Lincoln spun, searching for what, he didn't know. "Doc? Is this why?"

Doc caught his line of thought. "You think you took a picture and got something you shouldn't have?"

He nodded. "Could that be the reason?"

"I don't know, Lincoln. Let's get that officer to go into your home. It would be legitimate for him to go in and search. He did say you have a brother and sister. You should contact them."

Lincoln shook his head violently. "No, I can't. He'll hurt them."

38

"You have been adamant on that all along, even when you were semi-conscious. Okay. So we leave it. Eventually you will need to contact them."

"And tell them what? Hi, I'm your brother. I hear you're my family. I just don't remember you?"

"It would be better than them not knowing. Holly's still searching for her father, whenever she leaves here. She told me one time she just wanted to know if he was dead or alive, and if alive, could he tell her why he walked away. Don't do that to your family."

Lincoln froze, his eyes on Doc before they slid shut. He finally nodded, blinking back tears. "Okay. If I send a letter, would that work?"

"It would, but it won't answer the questions they have. You need to be specific."

"And I can't mail it from here."

"No? You're sure? All right, then we'll figure that out." Doc shoved him down at his desk. "Here, my word

39

processing program is up, unless you want to write it out longhand."

Lincoln stared at the pen and paper in front of him. "No, I think computer. I'll sign it."

Holly stood in the doorway, watching as he worked away. Doc had found her pacing his backyard and with a quiet word of explanation sent her to find Lincoln, knowing the two young people needed one another. Lord, he prayed, protect them. Protect their hearts if it is not Your plan for them to fall in love and I see that happening on a daily basis.

Holly finally walked to Lincoln, her hand resting on his shoulder as she stood, her eyes on his face, seeing his concentration but also the pain he felt, the uncertainty, the unknown.

He looked up, blinking for a moment to bring himself back to the room. "Holly?"

"Doc said you needed a friend." She sank into a chair near him, her head tilted to watch him, curls falling from the clip she had her hair up in.

He reached and pulled at one of the curls. "Your hair is such a beautiful colour. I don't know if I have ever seen hair that colour before." He paused, another memory tickling at his mind. "But I think I did, somewhere."

"Did you?" She smiled, the smile lighting up her face. "Did you get your letter written? Doc said you were attempting to write one."

He nodded, a grim look crossing his face for a moment. "I did. It's hard, writing to someone you are supposed to love and protect, but can't remember. I just wish I could."

"Don't try so hard, Lincoln. It will come. Just let your mind heal."

He handed her the letter. "Will you read this? Please?" He was almost begging, he knew, as she started to shake her head. "Doc tells me you still look for your father. Would something like this help?"

She sighed, her eyes on his, reading something in them she wasn't quite sure of. "It might."

She dropped her gaze to the letter, note really, she thought. "You're sure you want me to read this?"

He nodded. "Please." He rose to pace, finally standing with his back to the wall, standing in such a way he could watch her face as she read. Lord, I'm in over my head, here in Cairn. I have no desire to go back to where they tell me I live, to Hope. I don't know that I want to even meet my siblings, and that is wrong. All I want, dear Lord, is to stay here, live a simple life, and maybe fall in love? Holly is such a precious lady.

Holly's hand shook slightly as she took the paper, not quite wanting to read private words but knowing that she had to.

"Dear …"

"You didn't put a name to them. You need to." She heard him sigh before he answered.

"I know. I forgot what Dougal said they were."

"Logan and Larkin, I think. He sent me a text." She pulled out her phone, finding the message. "That's right, Logan

42

and Larkin. Larkin is in between you two men."

She turned her attention back to the letter. "You can handwrite in their names. That makes it more personal."

"Dear Larkin and Logan,

"I'm sorry I left without saying good bye but something urgent came up, that meant danger to you two, and I felt it best to leave without warning you. Please understand that I am in hiding and that I will contact you when I can.

"Please don't look for me. I don't want you two to be in any danger. Whoever it is that is after me has threatened you two. I will do anything I can to keep you safe.

"Lincoln."

"Well?" Lincoln approached her, dropping back into the chair beside her.

She looked at him, appraising him, then back at the note. "It really doesn't say much, but that's what you wanted, isn't it? You don't want them to know where you are or that you can't remember them."

He nodded. "If it was you and your sibling was on the run and hurt, wouldn't you try and find them? That's what I thought." He watched her nod, seeing the sadness on her face. He reached for the letter and then an envelope, hesitating. "I don't know their address."

"Send it to your address. I'm sure it will get to them." She watched as he searched for his address in his wallet and then stamped the envelope. "Let's walk to the post office and mail it. If you don't do it right away, you'll change your mind."

Doc appeared in the doorway suddenly, shutting the door and locking it behind him, a finger to his lips as he turned around. He moved quickly towards them, pointing towards the exam rooms at the back. "In there," he whispered.

Lincoln grabbed for Holly's hand, pulling her with him. "Doc?" His own voice was low.

"Ssh!" Doc stood where he could hear the noise coming from outside the locked door before he finally turned. "There was someone out there looking for you, Lincoln." His explanation had Lincoln drawing in a sharp breath and Holly turning pale.

"They're still here?"

Doc shook his head. "No, I think they have left. But they know you're still in town. It's only a matter of time before they find you. Just what did you get us mixed up in, anyway?"

Lincoln jumped at Doc's harsh words, seeing the worry and concern on his face. "I wish I knew, Doc. Maybe I should just move on."

"They will only follow you, Lincoln. Please. Don't leave." Holly's soft voice caught at his mind and he turned, seeing something in her eyes that had him agreeing not to leave, not yet anyway, much against his own better judgement.

Doc just shook his head. It's happening, isn't it, Lord? These two are falling in love right in front of us. The village will be glad and will do everything they can to protect their Holly. Holly was loved by all in the village, despite her propensity to speak the truth in unvarnished terms at time, but her willingness to lend a hand wherever and whenever it was needed was what drew everyone to her.

Doc finally let them leave, sending them on their way to his own home, telling them his wife expected them to stay for dinner. Jake rose from where he had been laying on the sidewalk, a sheepish look on his face.

"Jake?" Holly's voice was frustrated. "Just what did you go and do this time?"

Lincoln began to laugh as he stared down where Jake had been laying. "He's brought you some flowers, Holly. Now whose garden did he raid them from?"

Chapter 5

Two months later, Lincoln stood in Holly's backyard, a camera in his hand, feeling more like himself than he had, if he only knew how he should be feeling. He was waiting for her to return from her work, Jake sitting at his side.

He dropped to a knee, camera pointing at Jake. "Just like that, boy. We'll give Holly a nice photo of you." Jake posed and then rose to come and lick at Lincoln's face. "That's enough. Now, where can I take some more pictures, boy? What would you like to see?"

Jake woofed and then led the way to the back of the yard, stopping to sniff at the small gate, hackles beginning to raise, a growl low in his throat. Lincoln paused, watching first Jake and then the gate before he moved forward, seeing dusty footprints. He pointed his camera at them, clicking away before he opened the gate and walked through, Jake pushing at him to stop him.

"Jake? What's up with you? You don't want me to go out here? Is that it, boy?" Lincoln reached to rub at Jake's ears, feeling the raised hair on his neck. "All right, then, boy. I won't. Let me call Dougal and have him come out. There's something wrong here that you sense, isn't there?"

Lincoln turned to walk away, feeling Jake's body pushing at him. "All right, boy. Let me close the gate. What's out there, fellow? Can't tell me, can you? I wish you could."

Dougal approached him an hour later, a grim look on his face. "How long were you here before you headed back there?"

Lincoln shrugged. "Maybe an hour. I was doing some research on my phone and then starting taking photos. Jake stopped me from going too far past the gate." He rubbed at the dog's side with his foot as Jake sprawled at his feet.

"There was someone back there, no doubt about it. I found evidence that they've been there for a while. Watching you, I would say. They were fifteen feet from the gate. If you had gone any further, they would have nabbed you."

Lincoln paled. "Any danger to Holly?"

Dougal shook his head. "Not at present. I would say they are after you and you alone right now. That may change once they realize you two are a couple." Dougal smirked as Lincoln shook his head. "You are too. A couple, that is. Everyone sees it. In fact, they are already planning your wedding for you."

Lincoln stared at Dougal, before he remembered to snap his mouth closed. "They are?" His voice rose to a squeak, causing Dougal to laugh even harder. "Does Holly know that?"

"Does Holly know what?" Her hand on his shoulder had him sliding his eyes closed and groaning.

Dougal was still laughing even as he tucked his pen and notebook away. "That the town is planning your wedding? I highly doubt that she did, but she does now. Listen. Stay safe, you two. Call if anything else comes up."

Lincoln gave a half hearted wave, knowing he had to face Holly and not quite sure how he would. Lord, now what? I want this lady to stay safe, but I also want her in my life. What do I do?

Holly slid down beside him, reaching to hug Jake who had stood up at her knee to greet her.

"Did Dougal really say that?" Lincoln's voice was low.

"He did." She began to laugh. "Now I know why all the looks and smiles and hints. He's right, you know."

"He is?" Lincoln was flabbergasted. "They really don't do that, do they?"

She nodded, reaching a hand to touch his cheek before she clasped her hands. "They do. They have good hearts. I've been taken care of by the village all my life. I guess that saying is true."

"And what saying is that?" Lincoln's arm came around her to draw her tight to his side.

"That it takes a village to raise a child. I'm sure I gave them all a few gray hairs. I just couldn't stay out of trouble."

Lincoln grinned at the consternation on her face. "I'm sure you did, without meaning to. You are loved, you do know that?"

She nodded, a tone in his voice catching her attention and drawing her gaze to him. "Lincoln?"

He searched her face, a hand brushing down her cheek. "You are loved, Holly, in more ways than one. I love you, have for a while now, but was afraid to say anything. I don't want to see you hurt. Someone was watching today, back behind your gate."

"I figured something was up with Dougal here." She sighed, her head coming down on his shoulder. "We can't live in fear, Lincoln. God does not want that for us. He has promised protection for us. You know that as well as I do."

"He has. I just don't want to be the one that brings trouble to you." His arm tightened. "But I do love you deeply."

"And I, you." Her words were stopped as he kissed her. When she could breathe again, she smiled, mischief in her eyes. "Does that mean I get to keep you after all?"

Lincoln's shout of laughter rang through the yard, startling the birds settling for the night and sending Jake racing around the perimeter, barking. "I guess it does. Now what?"

"Now what? I'd say supper. I'm starved, you know." She waited for his next kiss and then rose, heading for her kitchen. "Let me see what I can come up with."

"Knowing you, it will be a surprise. Let me help." He turned to call for Jake, seeing him at the back gate and hearing growling from him once more. "Come on, Jake. Supper."

Doc just shook his head when they appeared in his study later that night. "What took you two so long?"

They laughed as he stood and hugged Holly and then shook Lincoln's hand.

"You'll have your hands full, you do know that, son?"

Lincoln laughingly agreed, watching as Holly struggled with her emotions, sensing how hard it was for her, not having her parents at this point. "Doc? Can I ask a personal favour? Will you walk Holly to meet me?" She had turned to watch him, tears blinding her at his words.

Doc reached to hug Holly again. "I would be delighted to. I just wish your Dad was here, Holly. He and I were good friends. It saddened me when he disappeared like he did." He turned them towards the door. "Now, let's go find Martha. She'll want to know right away. I'm sure she's already making plans. Seems to me I heard something about a wedding dress the other night."

Martha stood, eyes alight with love for the young woman hesitating in front of her, before she reached to draw her to her. "I know your parents would be happy. He's a good man, love, a good godly man. He'll take care of you." She too began to laugh. "Does this mean you do get to keep him, after all?"

Holly laughed through her tears. "That's too true, Martha. Now, we still have to set a date but we don't plan on a long engagement." She sighed, sorrow on her face. "I don't have Mom's dress. She had kept it for me, but it was damaged when the roof leaked."

"I know it was." Martha drew her with her to the back bedroom. "Here. I never had a daughter. I would be honoured if you would even consider wearing mine. It's old fashioned now though."

Holly was shaking her head. "I don't care. I'll wear it. Will it fit?"

Martha assured her they would take care of that. "Now, about what's going on with Lincoln?"

"The man after him? We think he was back behind in the woods today. Jake alerted to something back there."

"That's not good. Maybe you should be moving to town."

Holly again shook her head. "I'm not moving from my home, not unless that's what Lincoln wants and he says no."

Lincoln watched as Holly interacted with Doc, Martha, and Ted, seeing how much she loved them and how they all loved her in return. He knew then he would never return to Hope, no matter how much he was pressured to. The journey he had set off on without any idea of why or where had turned him into a pilgrim, intent on living a new

54

life. Even when or if he remembered his own family, Cairn was his home now. His photos were starting to sell from his online store, earning him an income that he knew would grow. He was investing, planning for his future. He just didn't expect his future to start so soon. Neither one of the young couple remembered the danger that awaited them, nor would they have cared at that very moment if they had.

Holly paced the next day, moving from room to room in her house. Something felt off, and she wasn't sure what it was. She had called Dougal, who promised to stop by after work. And why hadn't she called Lincoln, he wanted to know?

"Dougal? Thank you for coming." Holly stepped back from the door. "I just can't figure out what is different."

"Just a sense or did you see something?"

She shrugged. "Just a sense, I think. You know how I've always been able to tell if someone has been in my space."

"I know. It's uncanny, that ability of yours." Dougal walked through her house, not seeing anything overt but knowing Holly would not have called him if she hadn't felt something off.

"I just don't get it, Dougal. Jake was home and in the house. He would have caused a real stir if someone had entered that he didn't know. I would have found evidence of that." She turned to stare at her back door. "He spends his day in the sunroom. If something disturbs him, I find cushions on the floor and sometimes my book knocked off the end table. That hadn't happened today."

Dougal straightened up from looking at the lock. "It doesn't appear to have been tampered with." He watched her as she paced once more. "Is anything missing, moved, whatever, that you can think of?"

She shook her head. "No. That's the funny thing. Everything is just as I left it this morning. It's just that sense of someone being in here." She turned, fear flickering in her eyes. "Can it be whoever is after Lincoln?"

"It might be. You need to take precautions, Holly. They are watching the house. That's a given. I found that evidence last night." He walked around the room, pausing to look at a photo. "Holly? When did you get this photo?"

"What photo?" She stopped beside him, her hand reaching out to grasp his arm. "That's not mine. And I know it's not Lincoln's. Where did it come from?" She reached for it, her fingers stopping short of it as Dougal's hand covered her. "Dougal?"

"This is what you've picked up on. Someone placed this, likely when you were home and had Jake out front or out in the woods with you. You need to start locking your door, Holly, when you're not in here or in the yard. At least for now."

She shivered, fear driving chills up and down her spine. "I know, but we've never had to do that, have we?" She wrapped her arms around herself and began to pace again. "Who would do that? And just who is that man?"

"It looks familiar, but I can't place him. Let me take it and see what I can do with it."

"Please. Get it out of here." She watched as Dougal finally drove away before she dropped to her knees, wrapping her arms around Jake. "Just how far will they go, boy? What message are they trying to send me?"

Lincoln found her an hour later, wrapped in a blanket in her swing on the back deck, and dropped down beside her, an arm around her drawing her close before he placed a kiss on her cheek. "Holly? What happened?" He tilted his head to watch her face. "You're so cold."

She looked up at him and he drew a sharp breath in at the fear he saw lingering on her face.

"Holly? What happened? Don't tell me nothing. Your face says otherwise."

"Someone left a picture in the sunroom. I have no idea when or who the man is that is in it. Dougal took it."

"Did he? That's good." He didn't say anything more, just started the swing moving with a shove of his toe. "What else did you get up to today?"

She shifted slightly, turning more so her back was against him, feeling content and safe in his arms. "The usual. Rescued a cat. Saved a moose. Led a horse to water and made it drink." She waited, a small smile on her face, knowing that he hadn't really been listening to her but that eventually he would hear what she said.

"That's nice. Sounds like you had a good day." Lincoln studied the woods around him, knowing someone had been watching. Then her words caught his attention. "You did what?"

Holly began to laugh. "It took you long enough."

He laughed as well. "I can see I'll never had a dull moment with you, Holly. That's part of who you are and I love you so much."

They sat for a while, content in the dropping dusk, quiet conversation between them. They had set their wedding for three weeks from then, but with the village taking over the planning, they had not much to do. The village folks had told Lincoln privately that they wanted to do that for them, that Holly had given so much to each of them without asking for anything in return. He had swallowed against the lump in his throat and said a quiet thank you, knowing that words were not necessary. He just prayed he would fit into the town.

They ended their night with their usual time of Bible study and prayer before he kissed her and walked away, heading back for the village. He didn't hear the soft footsteps following him, or see the man that walked past him as he stood for a moment at the village wishing well, his thoughts on what was happening and how he could keep his love safe. His prayers deepened to a petition for her safety. He could do no more, he knew.

Chapter 6

Turning from her desk two months later, Holly smiled as she saw Lincoln totally engrossed in his photo editing. She was glad to have him with her, even as they both pursued busy careers or artistic paths or whatever it was called, she decided. She moved silently from the room, Jake rising from his bed to pad softly after her and to the door. She grabbed a sweater. Fall had arrived and with it cooler days. She loved the feeling of the fresh crisp air of fall, but missed the warmth of summer. She stood for a moment, her eyes on the horizon, before they dropped to her gardens. She was just about finished the fall cleanup but had left it for another day. She sighed. Today was that day, she decided. She was restless and had no idea why. The thought that she was waiting for something to happen crossed her mind and she vigorously shook her head.

She moved with purpose through her gardens, finally reaching the back gate. She paused, her eyes on it, a thoughtful look on her face. Lincoln had wanted to install a lock on it, but she had refused. Now, she was second guessing that decision. Perhaps they should. But then again, whoever it was could just climb over it. Jake alerted at different times to the presence of someone back here, but they had never seen whoever it was. Lincoln had taken long walks with Dougal, Ted or Doc through the woods, trying to find whoever it was, or at least a hiding place, but had returned, shaking his head at her question. The person was hiding well, he said. They could find no real trace. Perhaps when the snow came, they would. Lincoln was more afraid then he would let Holly know, afraid that she would be hurt, that he would be harmed and unable to protect her.

Holly was concerned enough that she had questioned him as to whether they should move to town. He shook his head, knowing how that would make her feel, and told her no, they would stay where they were. He had answered in a similar vein one day when she asked if he had wished to have his family at their wedding. He had stared into the distance, his brow wrinkled before he turned to her, shaking his head, stating that since he couldn't remember his family or even how they had gotten along, it was likely for the best they weren't there. Holly had stuffed the concern and sadness she felt for him down into her heart, bringing it out at night to pray for him and for his siblings. Dougal had mentioned that he had a brother and sister, confirming what Lincoln had said months ago, as well as his parents still living in Hope.

Holly dropped to her knees, her hands reaching to pull off dead stalks from the plants and drop them into the wheelbarrow she had beside her. As she moved along to the garden, she frowned. No, she wasn't seeing things. There was a new rock in her garden. She hadn't placed it there. She turned on her knees, searching the area before looking over her shoulder at the house. Lincoln wouldn't have done that. He was adamant that he would not interfere in her gardens and would only help her when she asked.

She reached for the rock, moving it from where it had been placed, a frown her face, Jake crowding in close. She turned it over, her hands beginning to shake as she stared at the bottom of it before she dropped it as if it was red hot and then scrambled, tumbled, crawled away from it, a piercing scream wrung from deep within her. She was never sure afterwards how she moved. It just happened. She tumbled to the ground, her arms wrapped around her body and head, her knees drawn up. Jake scrambled up to her, his barks turning to yelps and then to whines as he tried desperately to get to her, his paws clawing at her arms, his nose rooting under them, trying to reach her face his tongue, finally belly on the ground, crawling up beside her as close as he could, whines continuing.

Lincoln had risen from his work, stretching, his hands almost touching the ceiling, before he turned, a smile on his face as he saw that Holly had quietly left him to work. He reached to save his work just as her piercing scream split the arm. He spun, his face paling, and then he hit the back door on a run, his eyes searching for his young bride, hearing the commotion Jake was making. He was across the lawn in a few long strides, on his knees, his hands reaching for her, not able to draw her into his arms.

He finally sat, pulling her up by brute strength, to cradle her close, Jake intent on being on his knee as well. He pushed the dog to one side even as he felt along Holly's arms and legs, and then tilted her face to look at it. She had a distant look on her face, not seeing him at all.

Lincoln reached for his phone, calling Doc and then Dougal, knowing he needed their help, but not sure why. He stood, Holly in his arms, Jake bouncing around him, as he strode back to the house, intent on setting her down in the house and checking out the yard. Her hands clung around his neck, not releasing when he asked her to. He sighed, sitting down in a chair, cradling her once more to him, not sure even then what had happened.

Dougal watched for a moment as Doc tried to assess Holly, hampered by her refusal to let go of Lincoln before he turned for the back door, Jake heading out in front of him and running for the back garden and the rock Holly had moved. Dougal searched the area, finally standing over the rock, staring down at it, a sick feeling in his stomach that Holly had found it. Pulling on gloves, he picked it up, staring first at it, then at the garden, and finally the trees behind. What kind of person did this, he wondered?

Lincoln stood watching for a moment before he moved to stand beside Dougal, his eyes on the stones, before his eyes slid shut.

"Who does this?" Dougal could hear the agony and distress in his friend's voice.

"I don't know, but I want him. You're sure you haven't remembered anything at all?"

"Only snippets, not enough to even get a sense of what I'm remembering." He angled his chin at the rock. "You think this is related?"

"I have no doubt about that." Dougal stared down at the picture taped to the bottom of the rock, red crosses through both Holly and Lincoln's faces, with the words, "You were warned", scrawled at the bottom. "Lincoln, we need you to remember. It might be a matter of life and death that you do."

"I know, Dougal. Don't you think I know that?" His tortured voice carried to Doc who now stood on the back deck, reluctant to walk away when Holly needed him. "But how do I remember?"

Dougal shrugged. "I've had conversations with Doc on just that. He can't give an answer as to what might work." He turned, seeing Doc watching them. "He said you may be burying something deep that you don't want to face or that has made you fearful."

Lincoln nodded soberly even as he turned to walk towards the house. "That is likely it, Dougal. Go ahead. Check into what you need to. Just don't ask me to leave here or leave Holly. That's not happening."

Dougal watched as Lincoln stopped by Doc, the older man's hand on his arm keeping him from moving past him before he turned back to his investigation. He would have to dig deeper now, he knew, not liking that fact, but knowing that it would mean both Holly and Lincoln's lives if he didn't solve it. Lincoln was digging into his past, but he hadn't said much, other than that one sentence to Dougal.

Doc studied Lincoln closely, seeing the worry and fear he was trying hard to hide. "She's coherent now, Lincoln. She's terrified, though."

Lincoln nodded, his eyes on the door. "I know she is. I just don't know who or why. And I wish I did." He looked at Doc, despair on his face. "Why can't I remember?"

"Our minds are strange things, Lincoln. What might not bother someone will drive another person to whatever vice they turn to in order to deal with it. Whatever you went through those months ago, whatever pain, fear, worry, that drove it deep into your mind. We can try to bring it out, but we likely won't be successful. It will have to work its way out on its own. That's what we're praying for, all of us."

"Me, too, Doc. I want this over and over yesterday." He paused, his eyes turned to the deck under his feet. "I just don't think I can go back to Hope. The fear that drove me from there rises up in me every time I consider going back."

Doc nodded. "I know it does. What if we had your siblings or your parents come here?"

Lincoln shook his head. "I have no idea if that is a good idea. Somehow, I have the impression this involves them as well, their health and safety anyway."

"I'm sure they are involved. We just need to know how." Doc turned and watched as Lincoln moved away without saying another word, his mind already intent on Holly.

He stopped as he stepped through the door, watching for a moment as Holly sat at the table, a hot drink cradled in her hands, Jake's chin on her knee, his eyes on her face.

"Holly?" He sighed as she jumped before he pulled a chair over and reached for one of her hands. "Holly? Are you okay?"

She shook her head. "I don't know, Lincoln. I just don't know." Her eyes were still somewhat shellshocked and dark, not quite focusing on him. "Who does that?"

"Dougal said he's looking into it. I've been trying to figure it out, searching my name and hometown, but not coming up with anything."

"I don't think you'll find the answers that way." She leaned against him, her hand on Jake's head. "We may have to take a trip there to solve this."

He studied their hands, not answering, feeling her other hand come up to touch his cheek, bringing him comfort as only that touch she gave could. "I'll think about it, my love, but somehow, I don't think we'd find the answers there. It's been what, almost six months now?"

"Something like that. When you were first here, you kept muttering something about a year. Do you know why?"

He shook his head, his eyes on her face once more. "I have no idea. I didn't say anything to explain it?"

She thought for a moment. "No, I don't think you did. That was about all I could understand. You weren't too coherent, you know."

He reached to hug her, his chin resting on her head. "I guess I wasn't, was I?"

Dougal could give them no new answers when he found them, other than to state adamantly enough was enough and he was planning of searching further, calling in favours with friends on other forces.

Lincoln thanked him as he walked him to the door, Doc having already left.

"Call me, Lincoln, if anything comes up or you remember anything." Dougal stared at the keys he was holding in his hand. "Just do that, okay?"

"I will. I promise." Lincoln locked the door, suddenly feeling very unsafe in his own home and stood for a moment, his hand on the door, before he turned his head to listen to Holly on the phone. He knew a friend had called her about a garden they wanted, and she was trying her best, but he knew that sometimes one's best wasn't enough.

Lord, where do we go from here? This is about the final straw. He, whoever he is, keeps invading our home and our lives. Can we just end this and end it now? Lincoln turned finally, his steps slow as he walked back towards his wife, his thoughts on what he couldn't remember. He stopped and turned, heading for the office and a pad of paper and his pen. He slid them onto the table beside Holly, sitting quietly until she set her phone aside.

"Lincoln?" Holly watched him intently. "What are you thinking?"

He shrugged. "I have no idea. But putting things to paper always helps me. It clears my mind." He paused, realizing what he had said. "How did I know that?"

"Likely because it's a habit with you. Habits are hard to break, you know." She leaned against him for a moment.

He nodded, his eyes on the hands she kept rubbing together. "Talk to me, my love. What is it you are not telling me?"

She finally nodded. "I just can't explain how I felt today, when I saw that." A shudder ran through her. "Who does this?" She sighed. "I know. I'm repeating myself."

"I think we will be." He picked up his pen and began to jot notes. "Tell me exactly what happened, how I was, when you found me. We've gone over this before, but I didn't take notes. I need to now. Anything I've said over the past few months that you can remember, tell me."

For two hours they sat, discussing what they had remembered, posing possibilities, before Holly rose, a glance at the clock letting her know it was almost time for supper.

"Holly?" She turned as he spoke, a question on her face. "Do you think I should go back to Hope?"

"I don't know, really, my dearest. Not at the moment. I don't think you're ready to go back."

He watched her closely before he rose and wrapped her in his arms. "You're right. I'm not. I'm not sure if I will ever be." They stood for a moment before Lincoln moved to reach in to the cupboard for their plates.

Later that night, he slipped out into the yard, Jake beside him, and roamed the perimeter, watching the dog closely but not seeing him alert to anything. He sighed to himself. Just what did he think he was doing, anyway? Did he really think he would find whoever it was and stop them? That was his prayer, God knew that, but he had no idea who it was or even how to find out.

Chapter 6

Shutting the door behind her, Martha walked slowly towards Holly as she moved in her kitchen. Something had brought Holly here that day, and Martha would just let her talk or be quiet. It was never easy with Holly. She had a well deep inside her where she stuffed her feelings and only brought them out briefly if at all. That was, her really deep feelings. She had a sense that Lincoln was drawing from that well. She could see the changes in Holly and that made her happy.

Holly stood, her arms crossed across her abdomen, staring at the calendar on the wall. They were well in February now, she realized. She would soon be gearing up her business into the busy time. This year, she was not looking forward to it as much or as eager to get started. She jumped as Martha's arm came around her.

"Holly? What brought you here?"

Holly shook her head. "I'm not sure, Martha. I am really not sure." She turned her head enough that Martha could see the shimmer of tears in her eyes. "I guess I'm just missing my Mom."

"I know you are, honey. Here. Sit. Tell me what's wrong." She stopped as Holly flinched at the light touch on her arm. "Holly? What happened?"

Holly sat before she buried her head in her arms on the tabletop and sobbed. Martha's arm was around her shoulders, feeling Holly flinch as she touched her, her heart lifting in prayer for her young friend.

"Holly? What is going on?"

Holly finally raised her tear-drenched face. "I don't know, Martha. That's the thing. We've tried and tried so hard to figure this out and it hasn't worked out. We still aren't any closer to knowing who it is."

"But that's not why you flinched when I touched you. What happened?"

Holly shook her head. "It's not what you think. Lincoln gets restless sometimes at night, when the dreams take over. He can't control his movements. I've tried waking him, but I can't. Last night, he hit my arm, without knowing that he did. I can't tell him.   It would devastate him to know that."

"But you must, Holly."   Martha sat back, trying to come up with an idea or plan for her friend.

"But you see, Martha?   When he's dreaming, or reliving the events before he came here, he says things.   I've been keeping track. I don't have enough to make sense of anything yet." She stared down at her clasped hands, her fingers whitening as she tightened them.   "He can't know, Martha.   He just can't know." She didn't hear the whisper of sound behind her or the muffled exclamation.

Doc reached to draw Lincoln from the kitchen, Martha nodding at him. He shoved the younger man into a chair in his study and then gently closed the door, coming to sit in his well worn desk chair, his eyes on his young friend.

Lincoln sat hunched over, his elbows on his knees, face buried in his hands, shudders running through him as he realized what had happened the night before.   He finally looked up, his face white and tight, agony in it.

"I didn't know, Doc. She has never said."

"And she won't, son. That is who she is. She'll take whatever anybody dishes out and not come back at them." Doc handed Lincoln the box of facial tissues, holding it for him to pull out some. He watched as the younger man swiped at his face. "And you can't let her know you heard her."

Lincoln stared at him, then twisted in his seat to stare at the door before he sighed. "No, I guess I can't, can I? We're not supposed to be here."

Doc gave a small grin. "No, we're not. So, how do we explain that we are?" Lincoln stared at him, finally catching the glint of mischief in the doctor's eyes.

"I don't know, Doc. You don't have any way out of here other than that door there."

"No, I don't. Martha will cover us. Come, let's head out. We should be able to sneak out." Doc snuck a peek at the kitchen, catching Martha's eye as she stood, making the two women a cup of tea. She shook her head in silence, concern on her face as she looked over at Holly.

"Holly?   What actually has Lincoln said?"

Holly stared up at her as she stood next to her, a hand on her shoulder. "I guess I can remember. I need to write it down."

Martha turned, pulling over the pad of paper and pen she had handy in the kitchen for her grocery list, turning to a fresh sheet. "Here you go.   Just start writing what you can remember, just as he said it."

Holly stared at the paper before looking up at Martha.   "That's important, isn't it? I never thought of it that way. Let me see what I can remember." She bent her head, concentrating on the words, not seeing Martha wipe at her eyes before she turned away.

Martha stood back, her eyes on the distance, as she listened to the sound of the pen as it moved across the paper, pausing as Holly thought over the words, finally shoving back the paper.

"All done?" Martha reached for it but Holly moved it away. "Holly?"

78

Holly just shook her head. "I can't show you. I have to show Lincoln. And I don't know how to do just that."

"Show me what, Holly?" Lincoln's arm came around his young wife, as he dropped a kiss on her cheek, before sliding down into a chair beside her, Dougal sitting on her other side.

"This. This is what you've been saying in your dreams, Lincoln." Distressed, she looked up at him, seeing in his eyes his concern for her. "Lincoln?"

He shook his head. "We'll talk, Holly. That I promise you. But, what have you here?" He read through her notes, a frown in place. "I've said all that? I don't remember it at all."

"No, you wouldn't. You were in a really deep sleep. It's only been the last couple of weeks that you've been so agitated." She leaned against him, needing the contact that brought, the comfort she sought coming from his warmth and his strength. "I tried to waken you at first, but I couldn't. Then, I just tried to remember what you said. Martha suggested I write it down. I hadn't been and I should have."

"And I woke you up, didn't I?" He looked past her at Dougal, handing him the pad of paper, before looking back at her. "Did I hurt you?"

She shook her head, then paused. "No, not really. Just caught my arm last night. But you didn't hurt me." She began to shake her head harder at his look of distress. "No, Lincoln. No, you didn't. It wasn't as bad as some of the times I've tripped over Jake."

He didn't say anything, just wrapped her in his arms, as he watched Dougal. "Dougal?"

"You've actually said a lot here, did you know that?" Dougal looked between the two. "Holly, you've always had a good memory. I would say this is almost word for word."

"Now what, Dougal?" Holly peered around at him.

"Now, I take this and see what I can discover. It will help. I was running into brick walls, so to speak." He looked down and then back up. "It will soon be a year, Lincoln. Isn't that what he gave you?" At Lincoln's nod, he continued. "I have no idea how you remembered that fact but not the others. Let me go through this and I'll be back in touch. Thanks, Martha, but I can't stay for a meal. I have an appointment I need to get to."

They watched him walk away before the older couple shared a look and then watched as the younger couple tried hard to settle down and make conversation with them.

Lincoln finally rose, his hand reaching for Holly's, drawing her to her feet, and then reaching for their jackets. "Doc. Martha. Thanks. Sorry. Neither one of us is good company right now."

"Not a problem, son. Take care of yourselves. I have a feeling it's coming to a head soon. It's almost a year, isn't it?"

Holly searched Lincoln's face before she spoke. "Something like eight to ten weeks or so, Doc. What happens now?"

"For now, we go home and we talk, my love." Lincoln's hand was tight and firm on hers, leading her through the village and to the road towards their home.

81

She pulled him to a stop, her hand on his face, bringing comfort to him. "Lincoln?"

He shook his head. "I don't know, Holly. I really don't know where we go from here." He stared down at her beloved face. "I wish I did. I wish I could send you somewhere you would be safe until this is over. I fear it is only going to get worse."

"God will get us through, my dearest. That's a promise He made. He never breaks a promise." She stood for a moment, a frown on her face as she watched a vehicle come towards them. Theirs was the only house on the road, so the vehicle had to have been at their home.

"Holly. Move behind me, please." Lincoln shoved her back, moving them to the side of the road, watching as the car passed them, the lone male assessing them before nodding as he drove past.

"Do you know him, Holly?"

"No, I don't, but he seemed to know you."

They watched for a moment before they continued their walk, Jake coming to meet them.

"I thought Jake was in the house." Holly was surprised to see him, even as she reached to rub at his head.

"He was.   I don't like this, Holly." Lincoln's phone was out and he was asking for help.

Dougal walked towards them at long last, a grim look on his face.   "The back door was pried open. I've asked Hank from the hardware store to head here with a new door and a new lock."   He opened his notebook, pen posed above him.   "Now, describe that vehicle and that man."

Chapter 7

Two months later, Lincoln headed into the local hardware store, searching for Holly. She had said she needed to stop there in the late afternoon, on her way back from a work site. It was still somewhat early to be working outdoors but with the warmer, drier weather, she had started another one of the many projects she had been contracted for. She told him she needed some items for their own gardens and would he meet her there? She wanted his opinion.

Hank looked up from the customer's order he was working on and waved, pointing towards the back of the store. Lincoln headed that way, searching the aisles for her, and not finding her. He frowned, standing with his hands on his hips, looking around. Now where had she gotten to? He headed back to the front, not seeing her.

Hank walked towards him. "Can't find her? She's got to be here somewhere. She only arrived ten minutes before you did. She said she wanted some new tools or something like that. She headed for the back. Let's take a look outside."

Walking back towards the store from the garden centre Hank ran, Lincoln stared around, his eyes resting on a car that pulled away from the curb. He shook his head. No, he hadn't seen Holly in there. She wouldn't do that to him. Her car was still parked in the lot out front.

Dougal stared at Lincoln, fear in his heart for his friend. "She was here and now she's not?" At their nod, he turned to search the store. "Hank? Did you look in the storerooms for her?"

"No, I didn't. I had no reason to think she would be there." Hank blanched and then headed on a run for the back of the store and the storerooms. "You don't think?"

"We need to search everywhere. If she's not in the store then she's disappeared."

Lincoln stood in the doorway of the final storeroom, watching as Dougal searched the room, stopping to stare at the floor and then looking towards the exterior door. "Dougal?"

"She was in here, Lincoln. That's her phone on the floor." He turned at the strangled sound from Lincoln. "Describe that car, Lincoln. I need to get a description out on it. I think you were right. She was in there."

Lincoln sagged back against the wall, his heart thudding in fear, his head shaking in denial. "It can't be, Dougal. I was right here. He wouldn't do that, would he?"

"Who wouldn't do that, Lincoln? Who? I wish you would remember. This makes it hard, not knowing who we are dealing with. Have you remembered anything at all?" Dougal stalked towards him and stood, hand on his friend's shoulder.

Lincoln just shook his head. "No, not at all. Where is she?" He turned, almost on a run as he headed for the front of the store and to her car, staring down at it before his palms slammed against the roof. God, where is she? How did You let her get taken? Why do this to her? I'm the one he's after, not her. God? Do You even care?

Doc watched him for a moment before he moved to stand beside him, not saying a word. Lincoln's head finally turned so he could watch the activity in the store, shifting eventually to rest his back against the car.

"Doc?"

"Hank called. He said you needed a friend." Doc leaned back against the car as well, his eyes on Lincoln, not the store.

Lincoln shot him a glance, one eye half closed against the glare from the setting sun. "He did? That's good." He turned away again, his eyes on the road. "I thought I saw her in the car, Doc. Why didn't I go after it?"

"Don't beat yourself up, Lincoln. You weren't sure, now were you?" Dougal stood in front of him.

"Dougal?"

"She's not anywhere around here, Lincoln. I'm sorry. We've searched, even brought in a dog. He tracked her to where you saw the car." Dougal held up a hand. "Again, Lincoln, you couldn't have known, now could you?"

Lincoln finally slumped against the car, his chin dropping to his chest, even as he shoved his hands into his pockets. "No, I guess. I don't know. I should have known."

His head raised, a tortured look on his face. "How do we find her, when we don't know who we're looking for?" He paused, as his phone vibrated in his pocket. He pulled it out, a frown in place. "I don't know this number."

Dougal reached for it, noting the number, before he asked Lincoln to answer it.

They could hear shuffling in the background, then a voice they recognized.

"Just who are you?" Holly's voice came through clear over the speaker. "What do you want with me? Oh, I see. You're not talking, is that it? Well, don't expect me to." Her words cut off for a moment before she spoke again. "You want me to what? Ask Lincoln to meet you? Tell him that he has failed in his commitment? Just what commitment is that, anyway? You need to be more specific than that. I can't help you if you're not."

They listened to more shuffling before the phone cut off. Dougal walked away, his own phone to his ear, before he turned, a disappointed look on his face.

"Sorry, Lincoln. I thought I could trace it, but we couldn't. It wasn't quite long enough. What was Holly up to?" He watched as Lincoln struggled to bring his emotions back under his control, nodding when his friend finally looked at him, a grim look on his face.

"She was trying to help. Now, whose phone did was it that she had?"

"Not one we could trace very well. It's not from our area, that's a given. Not with that area code. Marge is working on that. Doc?"

Doc looked up, his face a mixture of emotions. "That's an area from overseas, if I'm not mistaken. Now, why does that ring a bell?" He shrugged, not sure where his thoughts were going. "Lincoln, come with me."

Lincoln shook his head. "Thanks, Doc, but no. I need to get home. She'll be looking for me there, if anywhere. Besides, I need to see to Jake." Lincoln walked away, shoulders slumped, a dejected look to his whole demeanour.

"Where is she, Dougal?" Doc knew Dougal hadn't said everything.

"I really don't know, Doc. I wish I did. I'd go bring her home if I could." Dougal watched Doc walk away, then headed for his car. He followed Lincoln from afar, watching carefully that no harm befell him.

Lincoln paced the house, Jake matching his steps. It had been two days, two days since Holly had disappeared, two days since his world crashed in on him. He hadn't been able to sleep. He had tried. God knew he had, but every time he closed his eyes, he could hear Holly's voice on that strange call. Where is she, God? Is she safe? Is she alive? Please, please, bring my love back to me.

He looked up as his doorbell rang, noting the time for some reason, then heading to open it, shock on his face, before he reached for Holly, sweeping her into his arms and slamming the door shut. He sank to the floor, his wife cradled tight in his arms, Jake whining and trying his best to get at Holly's face, licking at her arms, hands, at Lincoln. His whines finally broke through the shock Lincoln was in and he shoved at Jake, rising to his feet, still with Holly in his arms.

"Lincoln?" Her voice was low. "Can you set me down, please? I need to stand."

He slid her to her feet, his arms wrapped around her. "Holly? What happened? How did you get here?"

She just shook her head. "I need to shower and get cleaned up. Please, Lincoln. Grant me that. Then I'll talk. Please, don't call Dougal. Not yet. I don't want him to know I'm here." The pleas in her voice and the pleading look on her face had him agreeing, against his better thoughts.

"Okay, I guess. Here, let's get you cleaned up." He stood back as she shoved at him. "Holly?"

"Please, Lincoln? Let me be. I'll be right back." She walked away, not seeing the look on his face, the concern and pain there, before he looked down at Jake, motioning for him to go with her.

Jake slumped to the floor, muzzle on his paws, as he laid near the vanity in the bathroom, his eyes not moving from his mistress. He knew she was agitated and upset, and that something was wrong. His tail thumped as he wagged it when she turned, clean and ready to face Lincoln. She

91

sighed, dropping down to hug him tight, before shooing him out of the door in front of her.

Lincoln turned from where he had been standing in front of the window, watching the driveway, searching for how she got home. He just opened his arms and she almost ran to him, her face burrowing against him as sobs shook her body. He just tightened his arms, his heart raised in thankful prayer but with worry and question in his prayer as well.

"Holly?"

She nodded. "I'll talk. Then we have to make a decision, Lincoln. I'm still not sure if the man who took me is the man after you." Her brow wrinkled for a moment. "But the man who took me away from there is not the same man." She sighed, her eyes on him. "I'm not making any sense, am I?"

He gave a small smile. "Not really. Here, let's get you something to eat and drink. Then we will talk." He heard a sound out front and sighed as he looked. "Dougal's here."

She panicked, running for the bathroom and slamming the door. "Not yet,

Lincoln. Don't let him know I'm here. We have to talk first."

Lincoln stared after her, then at the door as the doorbell rang. Torn, he wasn't sure who he should listen to, finally listening to his heart and moving from the window towards the bathroom door, ignoring the knocks on the door, praying that Dougal would forgive him.

He tapped at the door, watching with a slight smile as it cracked open and he could see one eye of his wife before she opened the door all the way, craning to see past him.

"I didn't answer the door, though I should have. Now, let's get some food into you. Are you hungry?"

She shrugged, as she stepped into his embrace, Jake standing up to lick at her face. "I'm not sure. I'm just really tired. I didn't sleep the whole time."

"You didn't sleep for two days? Then we feed you and you sleep. We can talk later." He sat her at the table and turned away, stopping as her hand caught his. "Holly?" He turned back, assessing her.

"No, we need to talk. We need you to remember, Lincoln. And I'm not sure how we can do that."

He studied her closely. Turning, he walked towards the fridge before he spun, his mouth open to speak, to find her with her head on the table, her eyes closed. He walked softly back towards her, a hand going out to touch her hair before he reached for her and sweeping her into his arms, carried her through to their bedroom, laying her down and pulling a blanket over her. He sat in the armchair he had pulled close to the bed, his eyes on her, watching as Jake carefully jumped on the bed, laying tight to his mistress, chin on her neck, his eyes on Lincoln, just waiting to be told to get down.

"Not this time, buddy. This time, you can stay. Keep watch on her. That's what you're up to, isn't it? You won't let her out of your sight, not for a long time." He heard the whisper of Jake's tail as it moved before Jake reached out his tongue and swiped it across Holly's face.

Four hours later, Holly roused, her eyes opening in fright before she sank back on the bed. She hadn't been dreaming after all. She was home and safe. Lord, I have no idea what happened or who that man was. He seemed to know me, wanted to talk to me, but didn't. I feel like I should know who he is. It really doesn't matter, now does it, Father? You know. You sent him.

She swung her feet to the floor, waiting for the dizziness she expected to come that didn't before she stood, her hands reaching to twist her curls up on her head in a clip. She stared at her feet and then smiled. Lincoln had added a pair of his socks to hers, knowing she would have cold feet. She thought she remembered Jake laying beside her, knowing he wasn't to be on the bed, but bringing comfort as only he could.

She stood for a moment, her eyes on the kitchen table before she turned, finding Lincoln in the living room doorway, watching her closely. A smile lit up his face as she moved to him.

"Did you have a good sleep?"

She nodded. "I did. I wasn't supposed to, now was I? That was our agreement. I ate, we talked, I slept."

He just hugged her tight. "Your body said otherwise. It's okay. We can stay up all night if you need to." He turned her for the kitchen. "I have some soup and sandwiches ready. Jake let me know you were waking up."

"Jake. Yes, you, Jake. What were you doing on the bed, boy?" She bent to hug him, ruffling his ears as he whined and licked at her face and hands.

She sat back finally, watching as Lincoln moved their plates to the sink and then set a fresh cup of tea in front of her before he sat, a mug of coffee in front of him, and reached for her hands, his warm and strong on hers. Their heads bowed, he petitioned for wisdom, for strength, for peace, for hope, for whatever it was they needed at that point.

He finally reached to kiss her, his hand lingering on her neck, his eyes searching hers. "Tell me, my love. Tell me what happened."

She shook, her hands trembling under his. "I'm still not sure what all happened. If you use let me say what happened and then we can talk." He nodded knowing that what exactly what he had to do.

He shifted his chair closer to her, his arms wrapping around her, her head pillowed on his shoulder. He waited as she drew in a deep breath.

Chapter 8

Going back to that afternoon, Holly's eyes slid shut as she tried to sort through what had happened. She shuddered once more, feeling the arms that had entrapped her and the hand that had covered her mouth to still her cries for help.

She had stood with the homeowner of the project, going over the last minute details that they had agreed on. She was pleased with the reaction to her drawings. The landscaper had stood on her other side, reaching for the drawings and nodding. He could do this, he said. With the few changes that were needed, it would be done in no time.

She stopped to raise her face to the sun, her eyes closing as she felt the warmth, knowing spring had arrived. She was happy, she decided, happy in her work and more than happy and content with her life. Or at least she would be if Lincoln could only remember what it was that had happened. Regardless of that, she was moving on, doing just what her mother had asked her to.

Her mother had wanted her to find someone to love and who would share her passion for God and life. That she had done.

She slipped from her car in the front parking lot of Hank's hardware store, a smile on her face as she remembered how he had taught her the tools of her trade, how to use flowers and hard materials. He had been the mentor she needed. She waved at him as she walked in and headed his way.

"All done for the day?" Hank's grin was wide.

"I am. I need to look for some new tools for home though. The ones I have are starting to wear out."

"You know where they are. And I have new edging and patio stones out back to show you when you have a moment."

"Oh? You do? Terrific. Let me finish what I need to find and then I'll come looking for you." She grinned as he waved her away before turning back. "Lincoln's supposed to meet me here in about fifteen minutes."

"Not a problem, Holly. I'll send him to find you."

Holly searched through the tools, setting aside the few that she felt she needed. She turned, her eyes searching for Lincoln and not seeing him yet. She sighed. She had become used to being half of a couple. When he wasn't with her, she sometimes felt lost. How had she been able to function without him in her life? That was a question she couldn't answer. Not yet, anyway.

She turned towards the pet supplies, wanting to find something for Jake, but not sure what. She stood, her back to the doorway to the storeroom, not really registering the creak of a hinge. Her hand poised over a toy, she paused, listening, sure she had heard a sound. Then shaking her head, she turned back to the toys, a stuffed duck within her reach as she felt arms encircle her body, trapping her arms tight to her, and a hand coming over her mouth, stifling her startled cry. She was dragged backwards into a storeroom, the man holding her listening intently. She struggled to escape her captor, unable to bite his fingers though she tried. Unable to free her arms no matter how she twisted and turned. This was not Lincoln. He would not treat her this way. She couldn't scream, couldn't escape. She could vaguely hear Lincoln calling for her before his voice faded away and then became louder again as he talked with Hank. The man holding her waited and then picked her up, carrying her through a back door to the front of the store, setting her back on her feet, one arm still around her waist, the other over her mouth. She was propelled to a vehicle by the curb, shoved inside and the door slammed. She frantically reached for the other door only to be pulled back and her hands bound. She twisted, searching for Lincoln, seeing him but not able to signal to him that she needed help.

She slumped down in her seat, terror running through her. She watched closely as she was taken from her village and to a small house not far from town. She frowned. She knew this house, knew the homeowners. In fact, she had designed their garden. Why would they want to kidnap her? Because that was exactly what had happened to her. She had been kidnapped. God, she cried, please, let me escape somehow. Protect Lincoln, please, dear Lord.

She reached quietly for the man's phone he had set on the seat and dialled Lincoln's number, hiding the phone so it couldn't be seen. She questioned what the man wanted but he didn't respond with anything, finally searching for his phone and pocketing it.

She was roughly dragged from the vehicle and shoved up the stairs to the house. Once inside she was shoved into a chair in the living room. She searched the room, not seeing the owners and she frowned. Something was off here. She searched her memory and remembered. They were away for some months, as was their custom. Someone was using their home and that wasn't what she knew they liked.

She stood, intent on leaving, but was stopped by the man who had grabbed her. Roughly, he shoved her back down, this time releasing the bonds on her hand to tie her to the chair. She struggled against that, but his strength won out. She sat back, glaring at him, anger and fear waging inside her even as she prayed for release.

She heard footsteps behind her and froze in her movements. Who was it, Lord? Who had taken me?

"Your man is not cooperating with us." The voice was polished, articulate.

She twisted to try and see who it was but a blow to her face stopped her movements and she tasted blood in her mouth. Great. Get them mad and get beat up. Way to go.

She stopped listening to the man, her eyes searching for a way to escape. Finally, she heard his steps move away and the man who had bound her left too. She twisted her arms, not succeeding in freeing herself. She frowned. There was something wrong here. How was she to get away and get to Lincoln? The man hadn't wanted her, he said. He wanted Lincoln. Since he couldn't get to Lincoln, he took her. That didn't make sense. What was it he said? What was it he wanted Lincoln to do? She couldn't remember. In fact, she had stopped listening to him, just hearing a drone of words. That wasn't good. Lincoln, what is it you didn't want to do? It had to be something big.

Darkness had fallen when she was finally released from the chair and shoved into a bedroom. She spun as she heard the door lock snap into place and then was at the window. She couldn't drop down from the second floor. She just couldn't do it. She slumped to the floor, her back to the wall, her eyes on the door. She would not sleep, not until she escaped. But would her body allow her that?

The following morning, she was once more dragged from the room to the chair in the living room and bound in it again. She waited, for what she wasn't quite sure. She heard the footsteps from the night before and listened closely, her mind clearer as to what she had to do.

"Your man, my dear. He needs to cooperate with me. And he's not. You won't go home until he does."

She watched as the man came around her to stand in front of her. She frowned at him, realizing that she didn't know him. She heard his voice, her mind storing away his words even as she worked at trying to think of who he was. When he left, she slumped momentarily in her chair, then straightened, knowing she wouldn't be going anywhere but still searching. She thought about the man, something sending a memory to the surface. Did she know him after all?

Locked back into the bedroom, she paced, watching as the sun's rays lengthened and then shortened and night fell. She refused to close her eyes, refused to sleep. She couldn't, she decided. She needed to stay awake, to watch and try and get away. She tried the door numerous times, finding it locked. She prayed, her prayers at first frantic petitions for safety and release which grew to ask for peace, for understanding, for strength, for protection for Lincoln. She would not be defeated, she decided.

The next morning, the scenario was repeated but this time she was left in the living room. She heard the doors closing and then silence. She tugged at her hands, not able to get away. She heard quiet movement after a couple of hours and then a man appeared.

She gave a small scream, he had startled her. With a finger to his lips, he reached into his pocket for a knife, quickly slicing through her bonds and then grabbing at her hand, leading her from the house and towards the village, keeping to the shadows of the trees.

"Who are you? Why did you do that?" She questioned him, her voice soft, but received no response other than a shake of the man's head. "Do I know you? You seem familiar."

The man finally turned, his face shadowed by the grey beard and the cap he pulled down low over his eyes. A finger to her lips, he shook his head. A rough voice answered her.

"You may, but you need to be silent. I can't hear if someone is following us unless you are." He watched around them and then led her through the trees surrounding the village.

"Why not through the village? The people there will help us."

He shook his head. "I know, but word will get out too quick that you're free. You and your man need to leave here."

"We can't."

"No, you won't. There's a difference, isn't there?" His voice was rough from disuse but she still felt she should know him, had met him at one time.

"Are you sure we don't know one another? I think I do know you." She stood at the end of her driveway, watching him back away, his head shaking.

"Forget you've seen me." He was gone before she could even say thank you. She hesitated, wanting to run after him, wanting to run away from the village, but most of all, just wanting to run into Lincoln's arms and feel safe once more. The latter won and she ran for the door, falling into his embrace as he stood for a moment before reaching for her

She finally looked up at Lincoln, her thoughts coming back to the present, watching his attempt to control his features. Her hand came up to touch his face, bringing calming to him. His eyes on her, his mouth opened and closed, but he couldn't speak.

"Lincoln?"

He could hear the love and concern in her voice even as he bent to kiss her. "Oh, my love. We need to find that man. He saved you."

She nodded. "I know he did. But he doesn't want thanks. I know that. I would like to know why and who he is. I know him. I am sure I do." She yawned, her head settling against him. "I'm so tired. I can't think straight any more."

"Not sleeping for over two days will do that to you." He scooped her into his arms and headed for their bedroom, tucking her into bed despite her protests she wasn't ready for bed. "Sleep, my love. I'll be right back." He stood for a moment watching as her eyes closed and her breathing evened out as she slipped away into slumber before he raised his eyes, a fine anger showing on his face. Then he sighed. He had no idea who to be angry at. That he needed to rectify and just how he could do that, he wasn't even sure.

He sent Dougal a text message, knowing he would not be happy with either one of them. He was right. Dougal told him off, then asked if Holly was okay and did they need Doc to stop by? If not, he would be there in the morning, and they would talk.

Dougal turned from shutting the front door the next day, his eyes on Lincoln.

"Lincoln?"

"She's in the back yard, Dougal. Before you say anything, I made the decision not to call you in. She had not slept for over two days. She refused to, she said. But she also said she thinks she knows the man who rescued her."

"She does?" Dougal's eyebrows shot up and then back down. "How do we get her to remember?"

"We don't. We let it go, my friend. Trying to force someone to remember doesn't work. I'm a prime example."

"I know you are. Listen, it's coming up to a year since you appeared here. You have remembered nothing?"

"Nothing substantive. Nothing that would help. And before you suggest my going back to Hope, Holly and I have talked about that. We will if we have to, but I would rather not."

Dougal nodded. "All right. There's that then. Now, let's go find Holly and see what she has to say." He paused. "Are you sure you don't need Doc?"

"For now, I am. Here, Jake. Go find Holly." Jake took a look at Lincoln and then raced to find Holly, leaning against her as hard as he could. The two men could hear a bit of laughter from her.

"She's laughing?" Dougal shook his head.

"She is, Dougal. She's already shut away what happened. She will refuse to deal with it. I can't have that. She has to face it and won't."

"That she will do, my friend. Holly? What's this about you going on an adventure and not telling us?"

Holly started and then turned, her eyes on her friend before they moved to Lincoln, who smiled and nodded, his arms encircling her when he reached her. Dougal watched the couple, knowing just how deep their love had become, given what they had already faced. A shudder ran through him. They weren't done, of that he was convince, and he so wished they were.

Holly went back through what had happened, not able to give much more than what she had told Lincoln the night before. Dougal pushed for descriptions of the men and those she gave as best she could.

She paused. "How did they know where I was that day? I don't remember seeing anyone following me, and I have been watching, trust me."

Dougal shrugged. "A question we can ask once we find them." He paused, his eyes on Jake laying on Holly's feet. "It goes without saying you two are a target and need to stay safe. I still think we need to get you back to Hope. Or at least bring your family here, Lincoln."

Lincoln shook his head. "We can't. We have no idea what danger that would place them in. I don't want anyone hurt because of me."

"I'm sure they've been watched over the last eleven months. That's what I would do, to see if you had contact with them." With a final word of warning, he walked away, leaving Holly staring after him before her eyes raised to her husband.

"Dougal's right, you know. We need to face this. Then maybe your memory will return. You've been remembering more and more, but it's in bits and pieces and I can't make sense of it."

"And neither can I." His arms tightened around her, desperate to keep her safe but not knowing just how to do that. "So, what are we up to today?

"You have your photos you need to finish. I know you didn't do that when I was away. I have to check my work emails and see what waits for me. Life goes on, my dearest, whether we want it to or not. That's all we can do, keep moving forward, keep alert and trust God."

"Trust God? Do you know how hard that has been?" He turned her towards the house, their steps slow as they walked that way. "I try, but some days it's not there."

"And God knows and understands." She hugged him tight, her face against his chest, listening to his heart beat. "I just wish it had been different, Lincoln. We have this cloud hanging over us. What happens when it's gone? What will we find out?"

He stared into the distance, emotions warring on his face and in his heart. "I have no idea, my love. I am just so thankful you are with me. I could not face this without you, that much I know." He turned her to face the back of the yard. "Now, what were you thinking? You want to change something here, don't you?"

She nodded. "That I do. I'm just not sure what. Any idea I had is gone now, just like the wind." She paused, a thought crossing her mind. "Lincoln, can we place an ad in the Hope newspaper, telling whoever it is to leave you alone?"

He grinned. "I would if I thought that would work. It's a good idea. What would you say in it?"

She shrugged as she moved away, her eyes on her garden, her thoughts already tearing the plot apart. "I don't know. Something along the lines of leave me alone, that I refuse to do what you want."

Lincoln stood, his eyes on her before they raised to follow the flight of sparrows as they scattered from Jake's approach, their chatter filling the air for a moment. "You might have a good idea after all. I do know the owner of the paper. He was a good friend of my parents."

"You've never mentioned your parents in all your ramblings." She spoke from where she had dropped to her knees, her hands already reaching for the weeds in the garden.

"I haven't? That's strange. I don't remember them." He sighed. "I am so tired of those words. I want to remember but something is blocking me."

Holly paused, sitting back on her heels, her hands suspended in the air, the weeds in them blowing slowly in the breeze. "Lincoln, could it be someone you know? Someone close to you? Is that why you've blocked it?"

He dropped to the ground beside her, a blade of grass between his fingers. "That's the conclusion I've come to, but I have no way of knowing who. I need the information from my home and my office. If they are even still there."

"I'm sure they are. Your family would not get rid of either until they knew for sure. At least, I wouldn't." She studied the weeds in her hands, a frown on her face as she tried to remember picking them. "Where did I get these?"

"The weeds?" Lincoln started to laugh. "You just picked them, my love. You're distracted."

"I am. Now, can we get Dougal to talk to that officer in Hope, get him to forward you any address books, photo albums, etc, that you might need?"

Lincoln shook his head. "Not this time. Dougal is right. I do need to head to Hope. I just have to work up the courage to do that."

"You're not going on your own. I will be with you. So will Dougal. Of that I am sure."

"I know he will. Let's plan that for about three weeks from now. That would be close enough to the year for the man to come out and face me. At least I hope it would be."

Chapter 10

Three weeks later, Dougal slowed his vehicle, pulling to the side of the road outside Hope before he turned to watch the couple in the back seat and then sharing a look with Doc. Doc had insisted that he had to come, why, they weren't sure. He just smiled, shrugged, and said God told him to.

Lincoln's hand tightened on Holly's, and she raised her hand to touch his face, calming him. They had asked Doc why that happened, why her touch on his face did that, and he had just grinned and shrugged, saying he had no idea but that the touch from someone you loved sometimes did just that. Lincoln was a case in point, and if he wanted to become a test subject, then Doc would be happy to indulge them. Holly had protested, laughing at her friend.

Lincoln's eyes shifted from staring outside to Holly, his head tilting so he could watch her face, knowing this was difficult for her. It was for him and it was his home town.

"Where to first, Lincoln?" Dougal's voice broke into his thoughts.

"My office. We can go in the back way. I have the keys. At least I hope they still work."

"Did you have an alarm system?"

Lincoln shook his head. "No, I didn't. I didn't think I needed one. I can't say whether one might have been installed in the last year."

"Then, hope it hasn't been. I know you want to get in and out and not be seen. Best pull that cap down further on your face. It will help hide you." Dougal grinned at the face Lincoln made.

Holly stood, her hand on Lincoln's back, as he unlocked the door to his office and then hesitated before walking in. "No alarm system that I can see, Dougal."

"That's good. Get what you need as fast as you can. I don't like the feeling I'm getting."

"Me, either." Lincoln headed for his office, stopping to grab a box sitting on the table in the kitchen. He swiftly gathered what he needed from his desk, hesitating at his lap top and then dropping it into the box as well. "Dougal? Did you tell that cop that we would be in and out today?"

"I did. He promised to keep watch and make sure no one disturbed you. All set? Then let's get to your home and get you out of here."

Holly watched as Lincoln took one last swift look around the office before he headed her way, his hand reaching out for hers. "I'm set, my love. I don't think there's anything else here."

She pointed to a photo. "Take that. It has to be your family."

He nodded. "I will."

Dougal headed away from there, nodding to a man who stood outside the building next door, knowing it was the officer, Gerry, he had been corresponding with. Following Lincoln's directions, he pulled into a driveway shortly, waiting for Lincoln to run to unlock the garage door and then pulled in, letting the door come down behind them. He wondered afterwards how

Lincoln could remember the way and which keys worked what doors.

"Lincoln? Are you sure about this?" Doc watched the younger man closely. He knew this would be stressful for him, that he might suddenly remember. That was the reason he had chosen to come, to watch his friends closely. His eyes sought Holly, seeing the stress she was trying hard to hide. He stopped by Lincoln, his head tilting towards the young woman. "Holly is really stressing this, son. She won't tell you."

Lincoln sighed. "I know she is. I just wish it was different, coming here." He reached for Holly's hand, leading her through the door into his kitchen. "I guess this is my home, my love. I don't remember it."

She looked around. "I like it, but it's not the you I know and love. Who decorated it?"

"I think my sister did, but I'm not even sure of that. Wander around. If you see anything you think you want to take, we can do that. Dougal? Did I see some boxes in the garage?"

"That you did. Let me grab them."

Holly finally stood, watching as Lincoln stared down at his desk, his hands stilled, before she walked up to him, her hand going once more to his back. "Lincoln? Are you ready? Dougal thinks we need to leave."

He turned, a bleak look on his face. "I am. This is all I want." He looked around. "I'm not sure if I will be back. I don't want to leave Cairn. Even if I remember, I won't come back. My home is where you are. Will be for the rest of my life." He dropped a kiss on her forehead, before his hands turned her to walk with him back to the kitchen.

Dougal and Doc watched him closely. "All set?"

Lincoln nodded at Dougal's question. "I am. Let's get out of here. I have no idea if someone will come by."

Dougal drove away, Lincoln's eyes on his house, not seeing the younger woman who had climbed from a car, who stood staring after Dougal's vehicle, a hand to her face, her other hand frantically dialling her phone, her body turning to watch the vehicle disappear. Lincoln's return had not gone

unseen, unfortunately.   Just where that
would lead one had to wonder.

Lincoln sorted through the last of the
boxes, breaking the empty carton down and
stacking it neatly in the shed, knowing Holly
was arranging things in the office to put his
belongings away. He stood for a moment,
his eyes on her, knowing how hard it had
been for her. There were some boxes that he
had chosen not to go through, that he would
leave for another day.

"Holly?"

She stilled, then turned, concern on
her face. "Lincoln? Are you okay?"

"I am. Thank you, my love. Today
would have been unbearable without you
there."

She nodded, her eyes on his, before
she pointed to a book. "What is that? It was
in your stuff from your house."

He walked forward, his hands tracing
the worn leather cover. "It was my Dad's
diary or journal. His prayer journal from
one year. He gave it to me. I used to read it
over and over, feeling close to him, and
finding strength and wisdom in it when I

couldn't talk to him. I think I have missed it."

She watched closely, then just wrapped his arms around him. "I don't remember my Dad. He disappeared when I was young. He was overseas and never came back. Doc says they sent out investigators but no one could trace him. It broke Mom. She wasn't the same after that."

"I can see that, if she's anything like you. I don't remember them and I should."

"That's so sad. You need them, not matter how old you are."

He sighed, knowing she was correct. "I know, my love. Now, what's on the agenda for today?"

She shrugged. "Nothing except relaxing. But I know you won't do that. You want to go through what you brought, to see if anything triggers a memory. Let me get us some sandwiches and our tea and I'll help you."

Lincoln nodded, his thoughts already on what he had brought with him. I didn't bring a lot, he thought. There wasn't much there that I wanted. I know I don't want to go back to law. That's a given. I have found what I want to do, right here with my beloved Holly. He reached for the photo she made him bring, studying the younger man and woman in there, knowing they had to be his siblings, but no remembrance stirring in him. Lord, they've been hurt as well. I just want this over. I sense that it's coming to a head, but please protect my Holly.

He sat at his desk, his fingers tracing the features in the picture, realizing how much the younger man looked like him. He could remember their names but not them and that grieved him. He prayed that they were safe, that no harm had come to them. Holly's hand running along his shoulder eased his sorrow and he leant against her as she wrapped an arm around him.

"We should let them know you are alive, my dearest."

"I know. I just don't know how to." He leaned back. "I guess going in like we did today was a coward's way."

"No, not at all. You had to have closure on things, since I know you won't be going back there. We'll call them. I sure

Dougal has made sure they know you are at least alive."

He nodded. "That he said he did. He spoke to the officer named Gerry." He paused, his hand stilling on the photo before he rose, frantically digging through the paperwork he had brought from his office. "Here. I thought I had something. This is Gerry." He held out a file with a photo in it.

"I've seen him. He's been in town. Now why?"

"Checking on me, no doubt. That's what I would have done, had I been him."

She paused. "I guess." She flipped the photo over, finding a smaller photo attached to the back. "Lincoln, who's this? He looks familiar."

"Let's see." Lincoln looked at the photo, pulled it away from the other, finding no notations on it. "I have no idea. I can give it to Dougal, see if he can work any magic with it."

She stopped his movements. "Let me see it again, please. He looks like one of the men who took me. But I can't be certain."

"Then why is it with Gerry's photo? Is he involved in this somehow?" Lincoln began to pace, his hands running through his hair. "We need to talk to Dougal. He needs to know."

"And we will. Not today. He's on patrol and I won't disturb him. Not for this. We can talk to him tomorrow. Now, what else is there?"

Lincoln stared at her for a moment, then shook his head, a smile crossing his face. Leave it to Holly to make a decision, set it aside and then move on. "I really don't know. I just think something is about to happen and I don't like the feeling I'm getting."

"Nor do I." She paused as she heard frantic barking from Jake and then a yelp of pain. "Lincoln?"

He ran for the door, pulling it open and then sliding to a halt, backing up away from the weapon being held on him. "Holly? Run."

She ran for the back door, yanking it open and racing for the fence at the back, knowing Lincoln would not have told her to run if he hadn't been afraid for her. She pulled open the gate, thankful for there being no lock on it, and ran, searching for a hiding place, finding a deadfall that she climbed into, cowering down, her arms around her head. She heard the running footsteps and the curses when she was not found before the men returned to her home. She raised her head, her hand searching for her phone, finding with relief she had service. She frantically called for Dougal, only getting his voice mail, leaving him a jumbled message before she turned to face her house, her fingers working to dial the main line for the police service.

She rose, cautiously working her way back towards her home, not sure what she would find. She stood at the back gate, seeing Jake laying motionless in the yard, before her eyes sought her house. She moved forward silently, stooping for a moment to feel Jake, relieved her dog was alive, before she rose and walked to the back deck, hesitating before she climbed the steps, her eyes searching for the men. Hearing nothing, she walked towards the door, ready to run if she needed to. She softly and slowly opened the door, her heard thudding, fear sending the blood rushing to her ears.   She walked in, searching for Lincoln, for the men, not finding the men. She stood for a moment, sensing her husband was still there, but not seeing him anywhere in the house. She heard the sirens heading her way, saw the flickering lights and ran for the front door.   She jerked it open, her hands going to her mouth before she ran for the yard, dropping down beside Lincoln, who lay, like Jake, unmoving, not responding to her voice.

Dougal's hands raised her to her feet and out of the way of the paramedics as they worked, hurried but careful as they assessed Lincoln, finally shifting him to a backboard, a cervical collar   around his neck and soft blocks against his head in place.

Dougal's hand propelled her to his vehicle and he shoved her into it, almost sliding across the hood in his rush to reach the driver's door.   When he had asked the senior paramedic about Lincoln's condition, he had just shook his head and stated they needed to move and move right then.

Dougal watched as Holly paced the waiting room of the local hospital, not able to sit and wait. Doc had arrived and headed for Lincoln, not to interfere but to be there as a friend. He approached Holly, pulling her to a chair beside Martha who wrapped an arm around her young friend.

"Dougal? What did they say?" Holly's pleading voice almost brought his heart.

"Not a lot, Holly. Just that he had been beaten and that they needed to get him here. They'll come get you when they can." He shared a look with Martha, then continued. "Did you two find anything in what he brought back?"

She finally sighed, and then nodded. "We found a file with that officer, Gerry's photo, in it. Lincoln had not got through it so I don't know what it was about. But on the back, there was a photo." She suddenly dug into her shorts' pocket. "Here. For some reason I was holding it when Lincoln told me to run. I stuck it away. He doesn't know who it is, or at least he can't remember."

Dougal reached for it, his hand stilling for a moment. "You have no idea who this is?" When she shook her head, he sighed. "He's from around here. Or at least he used to be. He left years ago. Martha, is that who I think it is?"

Martha reached for the photo. "Johnson Mack. That's who it is. His mother despaired of keeping him on the right side of the law.

"Johnson Mack? Is that who it is?" Holly tilted Martha's hand to peer at the photo. "That who it was. He's the one."

"He's the one who, Holly?"

"He's the one who grabbed me. It's been so many years and you and I were young when he left. What is he doing back here? And how is he connected to that cop?"

"Good questions. Answers I hope to find." He looked up. "There's Doc, Holly." As she went to stand, Dougal's hand kept her in place. "Stay, Holly. Let him come to you."

Doc's face was grim as he crouched down in front of his young friend, a young woman he considered a daughter. He swallowed hard, knowing it would be difficult to speak with her. He had volunteered to do that and Joe, the emergency room physician, had taken a look at him and agreed. He would do it, if Doc didn't. He knew Holly well enough to talk bluntly with her. Doc had just shook his head, reminded Joe of what the young couple had been through, took a last look at Lincoln, and then turned to find his young friend.

"Doc?" Holly reached to touch his face, bringing his eyes to her.

He reached for her hand, drawing her to her feet. "We need to talk, Holly. Let's walk. I think better pacing." He nodded at Martha and she rose, her hand reaching for Holly's. Dougal followed them, his eyes on the trio, catching movement off to the side, a frown on his face as a younger couple entered, hesitating before the man headed for the clerk, spoke for a moment before he turned to look for Holly and then returned to the younger woman, who was clearly upset at his words.

Chapter 11

Holly waited for Doc to speak, not sure of what she would be hearing, but needing to know what was wrong with Lincoln.

"Holly. I think Dougal told you he had been beaten?" At her nod, he sighed. "I won't spare you. I know you too well to think I could get away with anything less than the truth." He paused in his words, his arm around her shoulders. "You have always been like a daughter to me, since your Dad disappeared. Your Mom knew and approved. We had many a talk, your Mom, Martha and I."

She waited, knowing he wasn't just reminiscing but had a reason for what he was saying.

Doc finally spoke again. "She worried about who you would marry, what he would be like. She would approve heartily of Lincoln. He is definitely your other half, your soul mate. I have rarely seen such a couple as you." He paused again. "The good Lord knows the reason for what you two are going through, what drove Lincoln here. I also know that you two have found peace with what you've faced, that if Lincoln was never to remember, you would be okay with that. Unfortunately, it appears as if that is not to be. I don't know who it was, but we think Lincoln does. He told you to run and you did just what he wanted. He took a severe beating, Holly. I won't lie to you. He's hurt and hurt bad. Right now, we will likely be needing to take him to surgery to stop internal bleeding. He is in deep pain. You will find numerous machines and lines running to him and around him." He paused, searching her face, seeing nothing but concern on it. "He will be on a ventilator for a few days. The surgeon wants to sedate him, to allow for better pain control, to allow him to start healing."

"I understand. Can I see him?" Holly turned back towards the hospital from the parking lot they had been pacing. "Doc? Please? I need to go to him. He needs me."

"That he does. Come on, then. Let's get you to him."

Dougal stood for a moment, watching the people in the waiting room, his eyes drawn once more to the young couple, and frowned. They looked familiar but he wasn't sure why. He watched as Holly moved towards the door to the examination rooms, Doc's arm around her. Martha paused beside him, her quiet voice saying she was heading for the chapel, but that she had called their pastor, who was on his way in.

Holly paused at her husband's bedside, reaching for his hand, her other hand on his cheek, stilling his restless movements. She reached to kiss his forehead, resting her forehead there for a moment. She could see the pain Doc mentioned. Lord, heal him. Please, dear Lord. Heal him. Help us to find the men responsible. This can't go on for much longer. It's a year now, Lord. A year since his last beating. He can't take more of these. I'll lose him if he does.

She stepped aside as the nurse approached, then nodded as she followed her to where the surgeon was waiting, waiting to explain what he had to do, what she could expect, and handing over the paperwork for her to sign. Her questions answered, her heart in her throat, she signed, then stood, staring down at the clipboard, tears gathering in her eyes. The surgeon gently took the clipboard and stood, a hand on her shoulder, his head bent as he prayed.

Neither saw the younger woman who had entered without permission, searching until she found Lincoln's room and then walked to stand near his stretcher, her hands clenched at her side, tears on her face. The nurse gave her a sharp look and then looked towards the doorway, not sure if she should ask the woman to leave or if Holly had agreed she could be in there. She didn't know her.

Lincoln began to twist and turn, pain on his face, his breath coming in short gasps. The nurse couldn't calm him and ran for the physician, Holly heading her way. Holly took one look at the nurse's face and then ran for Lincoln, brushing past the younger woman, not sparing her more than a glance, before her arm was around Lincoln, her hand on his face. She felt his agitation easing, his movements stilling as he calmed. She kissed him gently, her hand on his face, knowing if she moved, he would become agitated again and they just couldn't have that.

Lincoln's eyes flickered open, not focusing on the woman who stood at the foot of his bed, a frown of displeasure and dislike for Holly on her face, before he raised his glance to the woman he loved more than life itself.

"Holly? You're safe?"

"I am, my dearest. I ran and hid, just like you asked. I'm sorry, Lincoln. I'm so sorry." She blinked back her tears, willing them to fade, as she watched closely, seeing past the bruising and the cuts. "Dougal found us."

"You called him." Lincoln's voice was raspy and low and he breathed in gasps of air. "It hurts, Holly. It hurts so much."

"I know, my dearest. They'll be taking you to surgery soon. They said you're bleeding and they need to stop it." She watched as his eyes slid closed and he nodded. "I'll be waiting for you. I love you."

She heard the footsteps behind her, knowing they had come for him, but not wanting to let him go. She heard his low, barely audible whisper of love for her before she stood back. The surgeon eyed her and then nodded, telling her she could ride up to the surgical suite with him but then she'd have to wait. She thanked him, once more brushing past the other woman, not seeing her, her focus on her beloved.

The younger woman followed, then searched for the stairs, running up them to the surgical floor, shoving through the door and to the waiting room, her eyes narrowed as she searched for THAT woman as she termed her. She had no business with Lincoln. That was her right. She didn't turn away as she watched Holly pacing at the end of the waiting room, barely moved aside as an older gentleman moved past her, a frown on his face as he looked at her.

The younger man she had been with finally found her, a hand on her arm drawing her to one side. She just shook her head at his words, wrenching her arm away and pacing to a chair, where she flopped down, arms crossed, eyes on the people as they moved around them. The younger man studied her and then turned his eyes to Holly, a frown on his face, trying to place her, to understand her relationship to Lincoln.

Holly finally sat on the edge of the window where she could watch the door to the hallway, knowing it wasn't time enough yet for the surgeon to come find her. Doc had been there, but had been called away. Martha was there, seated close to her, her eyes closed as she prayed. Others from her church had been in and gone. Their pastor was in the chapel, leading a group in prayer for them she knew. Hank was seated beside Martha, not wanting to walk away from his young friends. Dougal finally entered, his eyes focused on her, before he sat beside her, shoulders touching, the comfort of long time friends in the silence between them.

"Any word yet, Holly?" Dougal kept his voice low.

She shook her head. "Not yet. They said it would likely be a couple of hours at least, if not longer, depending on what they found." She leaned her head against him, her arm linked around his, seeking the comfort from a friend who had been so much like a brother to her over the years. "I'm scared. They really beat him."

"I know, Holly. Did you see them?"

She shook her head. "No. I wish I had. Then I could give you a description. Lincoln answered the door and told me to run. I did. I hid in the trees out back." She suddenly sat up, fear and horror on her face. "Jake? I forgot about Jake!"

"He's okay. Doc had him taken to the vet's. I guess they hit him and knocked him down, then sedated him." Dougal held out a bottle of orange juice. "Doc said to give you this, you'd need it."

Holly gave a half smile as she took it and opened it, staring at it before she drank. "He knows me too well, doesn't he?"

"He knows all of us that well. That's what makes him the doctor he is." Dougal's eyes searched the crowd, stopping once more on the young woman. "Holly, do you know who she is?"

"Who? Oh, that woman? No, I don't. But come to think of it, she was in Lincoln's room and she shouldn't have been. How did that happen?"

Dougal stared at her for a moment, then at the younger woman. "I have no idea, but I will find out. I promise you. I'll ask after I know Lincoln is back in a room. Did they say anything much?"

"I really can't remember, and I should. Doc said he'd talk to me after the surgery, when he could explain better." She sighed, her eyes closing. "Was it only this morning we went to Hope?"

"It was. A flying trip, I'd said. It's been a long day for you."

"And you. You did all the driving. How'd we do the trip in that short of time?"

He grinned. "You didn't see the escort?"

"Escort?"

"Yes, escort. We had an escort there and back and could travel a higher speed. That was all cleared beforehand."

She stared at him. "You did that, didn't you? I gave you that picture, didn't I?"

"You did." Dougal looked up at movement near the doorway. "There's Doc and the surgeon. Let's get you over to hear what they have to say."

Holly was on her feet, almost running as she approached Doc. "Doc? It's not been two hours? What went wrong?"

Doc just hugged her before setting her back, his hands on her shoulders. "Nothing went wrong, Holly. Everything went right. Dave here says there wasn't the bleeding they knew they'd find. He did have some. They've fixed it. We can go into details later. Right now, they're getting him settled into a bed in ICU. Then they'll come find you."

Dave, the surgeon, spoke up. "He is on a ventilator, just as we talked about, Holly. That should only be for a couple of days before we pull it. His oxygen levels aren't where they should be and this will help. It will also help as we keep him sedated to manage his pain. Remember, we did talk about that? I'll come find you when he's settled. We still need to talk."

Holly nodded, her eyes searching for Lincoln, finally seeing him wheeled towards a room. She moved that way, standing outside the room, her eyes on her husband, not seeing the activity around her, not seeing the couple from the waiting room, who stood down the hall from her, a questioning look on the man's face, almost hatred on the young woman's. Doc watched them, then moved towards Holly, an arm going around her.

"You'll get in soon, Holly. Just let them have a few moments. Dave's headed our way. He wanted to talk to you again."

She nodded, looking past him. She frowned. "Doc, do you know that couple? It feels as if they are following us. She was in Lincoln's room downstairs. I have no idea how she got in there."

"We'll find out. For now, let's move over here and talk to Dave. Dougal's here as well."

Holly moved away reluctantly, her eyes back on Lincoln, before she turned to hear the surgeon.

The younger man down the hall had moved away, back into the waiting room, but the younger woman had crept along the hall, watching until the nurses have moved out of Lincoln's room before she entered, to stand at the foot of his bed, her eyes on him, watching as he moved restlessly, his movements becaming stronger.

The nurse shot her a glance as she entered, her eyes going back to Lincoln and then she moved forward in an attempt to still him. She was unsuccessful and remembering what she had been told, moved to the hallway, looking for Holly.

Holly saw her and ran towards her, the physicians following. A few words from the nurse and she was in the room, focused on Lincoln, her arm coming around him once more, her hand on his cheek. This time, he didn't still but kept moving, tossing and turning, pulling out his IV line and his hand moving towards the ventilator.

Holly finally found the button for the bedrail and lowered it, leaning in closer to Lincoln before she looked up at the nurse and saw for the first time the woman at the end of the bed.

"She needs to leave. Now." Dougal was there, his hand out to draw the woman away, despite her protests that she had every right to be there. "Dougal. Get her out of here."

Holly's attention went back to Lincoln and when what she was doing from the side of the bed didn't work she climbed up beside him, her arm around him, her hand on his face. She didn't hear the continued protests and refusal to leave uttered by the young woman, which only stilled as she caught sight of the ring on Lincoln's finger and the matching band on Holly's.

Dougal finally reappeared at Lincoln's bedside, seeing the calmness of his friend as she tried to calm her loved one. He saw the effect of Holly on Lincoln and sighed. Doc was right. They are two parts of a whole. Only she could calm him enough and like that.

Holly's voice stilled in its low singing and words, her head cradled against Lincoln, her hand on his cheek, watching as he settled. She was tired, she suddenly decided, tired and dirty. She didn't care about the streaks of dirt on her legs or her arms or even her face, the scratches on her arms and hands and legs, the dirt on Lincoln's T-shirt that she had pulled on earlier that day. She only cared about him.

Chapter 9

It was late evening when she could finally walk away from Lincoln, knowing that his body had slipped away in the drug-induced rest the doctors wanted for him. It broke her heart to see him like that, but knew it had to be that way. She paused in the doorway, looking back, fatigue making her stumble. Had it only been this morning that we snuck into Hope and back out, she thought. It felt like weeks ago, but then Dougal had had them on the road by five in the morning, and back home by early afternoon. She smiled. He was such a wonderful friend, never asking if he could help, just there when he was needed.

She turned to the waiting room, knowing Doc was still there, and that she needed to send him home. He had been up for the same hours that they had been and he wasn't young like them. She slid into a seat beside him, hugging him, before sitting back, Dougal sitting on her other side. She looked at him and frowned at the anger he was barely keeping tamped down.

"Dougal?"

"Holly? How's Lincoln?"

"He settled for now but we don't know for how long. The nurse said he should not have been able to rouse like he had, not with the anesthetic he was given." She leaned a head against his shoulder for a moment, fatigue washing over her. "I won't be leaving here any time soon. Can you talk to Phil? He has the plans for the next few gardens. He can call me or text me."

"He said he would. I already talked to him. There is no problem there." He nodded across to the couple sitting there. "Now, that over there. That's a problem."

"How so?" She raised her head and squinted, the lights hitting hard on her tired eyes. "Do I know them?"

"No, but apparently Lincoln does. Only he can't remember."

"Dougal, you are not making sense, or else my brain is too tired." She heard Doc give a snort of laughter. "Just who are the?"

"Relatives of yours now, I would say." Dougal shook his head at her, a grin barely

145

hidden. "You're not catching on, Holly. Being slow like that? That's not you."

Doc gave a small laugh. "Easy, Dougal. Show some compassion for her. She's been through a lot today. Holly, what he's trying to say is that couple over there? They are Lincoln's brother and sister."

"They are? That's why they looked so familiar." Holly yawned, her eyes sliding shut as her head came down on Doc's shoulder. "Introduce me, Doc. I'm sure you've met them."

He watched with concern as she slept, knowing she needed it, and also knowing it would be unlikely she would get enough, that Lincoln would rouse and need her calming spirit.

Doc looked over at the other couple, seeing concern on the man's face, but dislike on the woman's and sighed. Lord, can You please make this easier for Holly? She doesn't need hostility with what she's facing. Her whole life has been upside down for the last year, and she could use some stability for a change.

Dougal watched his friend and then with a quiet word to Doc, walked away. He needed to be back on duty and hated to leave, knowing Doc would be leaving shortly.

Holly stretched out on the couch in the waiting room, her head pillowed on her arm, a blanket the nurse found her over her, and lay, her eyes closed, her heart in prayer, her thoughts jumbling into her prayers. She just couldn't go on, she informed the Lord. I just can't. I'm through my strength, Lord. The last year has taken any reserves I've had. To be told his family is here, that is not what I need. I know, Lord, I'm telling You what I need, but You know that much better than I do. A tear trickled down her face and she didn't have the strength to reach up and wipe it away. She finally rose, moving silently from the room, not seeing her action followed by the woman. The man slept, but the younger woman rose, trailing after Holly, standing in the hallway watching as Holly stood by Lincoln's bedside, her hand on his face, stilling the agitation he was feeling. She shook her head as Holly finally crawled up beside him and laid there, her arm around his chest, and slept.

The nurse looked askance at her, finally speaking to her, letting her know she needed to move from the hallway. The young woman finally nodded, but her eyes remained on Lincoln, concern flickering in their depths before she returned to the waiting room. Somehow she just had to get in to see him. She could calm him just as well as that other woman.

Holly looked up the next day as Dougal approached quietly, his badge glinting in the light from the ceiling. He shook his head at her, seeing the fatigue, before he handed her a knapsack.

"What's this?"

"Martha sent some clean clothes. Said you needed them. She's right. Go on. Get cleaned up. I'll meet you back in the waiting room. We need to talk, Holly."

She stared at him before nodding and heading out to find a shower, the nurse directing her to one. She was back in short order, her wet hair hanging down her back before Dougal growled at her, took her clip and twisted her hair up on her head, securing it, just as he would for his own sister.

"Thanks, Dougal. I needed that shower. Now, what was it you wanted to talk to me about?"

"Them." He nodded at the younger couple. "You can't avoid them forever, you know. You need to meet them and hear what they have to say."

She sighed, her eyes closing. "I know. I just can't, Dougal. I just can't do it."

Dougal prayed for wisdom, knowing he had to be firm with her. "No, that's not true. It's that you won't and you need to, whether you want to or not. They will be a part of your life, and have been, even though Lincoln doesn't remember them very well. I've talked to them. They have no idea what's been going on. Only you can tell them what has been, and you need to. At this point, their lives may be at risk as well as yours and Lincoln's." He watched as understanding filled her face. "Didn't think of that, did you?"

"We've talked about that, but Lincoln thought they would be okay if he stayed away from them. You're saying they're not?"

Dougal shrugged. "I have no idea, but you can't hide any more, Holly. You need to talk to them."

"I know. It's just so hard without Lincoln here, even though he doesn't remember them."

"What do you mean, doesn't remember us? Of course, he does."

Holly's eyes raised to the hostile eyes of the young woman and sighed, nodding as the man, or brother, she thought, approached. "Can you sit? This will take a while. No, Dougal, don't leave. You're part of this."

Holly watched as the woman finally sat, hostility radiating from her. She lifted up a prayer for wisdom and guidance, before shooting a look towards the hallway. She had no idea how long it would be before Lincoln would become agitated and need her. She was the only one who could calm him. The nurses had accepted that fact and let her stay.

She turned her attention to the younger couple, her eye studying them, seeing a resemblance to Lincoln, more so than had shown in the photo

"Hi. I'm Holly. You must be Logan and Larkin."

"Well, at least you know our names. That more than I can say for us. Just who are you and why is Lincoln here and not in Hope? That's his home." Larkin's voice was harsh.

Holly studied the younger woman, a year or two younger than her, she thought, and felt compassion for her. After all, her brother had disappeared and they hadn't known where he was.

"How did you find him?"

"Larkin saw you that morning and called me. She saw the Cairn insignia on the car door and dragged me here." Logan's hand on his sister's arm kept her silent as did the warning tone in his voice. "We had no idea he was here. We were looking for him and had stopped in the restaurant just outside of town for something to eat when we heard someone calling for Doc, I think they said, and that he was needed at the hospital and why. We followed over here and have been waiting to speak with you. Larkin's tried to get to speak to Lincoln but hasn't been able to."

"Yeah, because she kept me away from him." Larkin slumped back in the chair, her eyes on the floor, her arms crossed across her body. "I want to know why."

Dougal spoke up. "She's Lincoln's wife. They married, what eight months ago now, Holly?"

She nodded. "Today, no, yesterday was eight months." Her eyes never left the younger man. "You look like him, but I don't know you. I have no idea how you will take what I am about to tell you."

"And that would be?" Logan leaned forward, elbows on his knees, chin on his folded hands.

Holly drew in a shaky breath. "That is so Lincoln. When he's really listening to someone, that's how he sits." Logan and Larkin exchanged a frown.

"He's always done that. I guess I just copied him. But come to think of it, that's how Dad would listen to Lincoln and I. I guess we picked up his mannerism."

"I see. That could be." Holly paused, not sure how to continue. "I need to tell you how Lincoln ended up here and how we met, but I can't do that if you interrupt me. If you interrupt, I will stop talking and walk away. You will never get the real story. Only Lincoln and I know exactly what has gone on. Dougal, my friend here, and Doc know part but not everything. Can you do that for me?"

Logan nodded. Larkin opened her mouth to protest but snapped it shut at a glare from Logan. "We can do that, Holly, is it? We need to know. We've searched for him over the past year, never finding him until now."

"That's how he wanted it. He didn't want you to find him. He was so afraid for your lives."

"Afraid? How can that be? What did you get him involved in?" Larkin's voice cut through the silence that met Holly's words.

Holly drew back, anger briefly on her face. "Logan, rein your sister in or I will not continue."

"Larkin, shut up, will you? She means it. For once in your life, stop talking and listen." Logan spun in his seat to glare at his sister. "If you can't, then walk away. I, for one, want to hear what she has to say."

Larkin opened her mouth to protest, then snapped it shut, a hard nod of her head meeting his words. Logan paused long enough to ensure she would be quiet before he spoke. "I apologize, Holly. Will you continue?" He turned back to watch her.

She struggled with her emotions, finally taking a deep breath. "As I asked, I have to tell you without any interruptions. Lincoln can't speak for himself and he should be the one telling this, not me."

She sank back in her chair, her eyes on her folded hands, fear briefly on her face. "It began a year ago today, actually. Lincoln showed up on my doorstep, beaten and unconscious. He couldn't remember his name. We had to tell him that. We searched for any note, any card that would give up a name of a relative, but he had nothing in his wallet, just his driver's license and a credit card and that's about it. We had no idea where he came from other than his address in Hope. He had no phone. No luggage. When he finally awoke, he couldn't remember anything, other than he was afraid. Over the course of the last year, he has remembered bits and pieces but nothing concrete enough that we can act on. He has given us no name as to the ones who beat him up. All he could say was that he was asked to do something and he refused. That he had been given a year and he still wouldn't agree. We don't know what he was asked to do, who asked, or if anyone else was involved. We married about eight months ago. And before you ask, Dougal checked him out, reassuring us that he had no girlfriend, fiancee or wife that he didn't remember. He spoke with an officer named Gerry in Hope. We were back there yesterday as Lincoln and I decided that we needed to see where he worked and where he lived, to try to find anything that might help us solve this mystery and move on. And before you ask, about a month ago, I was kidnapped, likely with the whole intent to make Lincoln do what they wanted, whoever they are."

Logan had watched intently, his eyes not moving from her face. "That explains why he didn't come home. He's like that, very much concerned about others. I can tell you love him deeply. If you love him that much, then I know he returns that love. And Gerry was right. Lincoln never dated, never wanted to. He had been busy setting up his law practice. There has been talk of his taking over as a judge, but he never seemed interested in that. In the last year or so before he disappeared, he was restless. Law didn't seem to be taking his whole attention any more. When I pressed him on it, he couldn't say why." He looked at Larkin when she made a sound. "He didn't tell you that, did he, sis? He didn't want you to worry about him, and you know you would have."

Larkin nodded. "I would have. It doesn't explain what happened though. How did he end up in this town? It's not what he's been used to or what he said he wanted."

"Larkin, you're cutting close to being rude. So stop, already, will you?" Logan was losing patience with his sister. He turned back to Holly, finding she had left.

"She won't put up with that, you know." Dougal sat forward. "Your arguing like that? She walked away. And if you continue like this, she will ensure that you don't see Lincoln until he can decide for himself. She has that power." Dougal held up a hand as Larkin opened her mouth to protest. "That's what I'm talking about. What you're about to do. You walked into the rooms without permission last night. You could be banned for just that, for attempting to interfere in his care."

"He's right, Larkin. For once, you need to think through your actions."

Larkin glared at her brother, meeting his calm facade and knowing he was right. "What is it with you? We're family. Of course we can go in and see him."

Dougal's snort caught her attention and she spun to stare at him. "That's not how it works. She has final say, after the doctor's word. If they say you don't go in, you don't go in. That's life. Face it. You have been hostile to someone I care about as a sister, and I won't put up with that attitude. So lose it or lose access to Lincoln." Dougal rose and walked off to find Holly, leaving the brother and sister arguing.

Holly stood where she could watch the siblings, knowing Dougal had stopped beside her. "Did she really just do that, argue with me?"

Dougal sighed. "She did. He's level headed. Pray he talks some sense into her. Lincoln doesn't need the family drama."

"No, he doesn't. I intend to make sure that doesn't happen, until he's able to make the decision himself." She reached up to hug her friend. "Thank you, Dougal. I just pray you find someone to complete your heart." She walked away with that, leaving him staring after her, a puzzled look on his face, before he heard a sound and turned to find Larkin near him, a thunderous look on her face as she stared at first him and then after Holly before she stomped off after her. Dougal bit back a grin, knowing that for once the princess as he had come to call her wouldn't get her way.

Holly heard the footsteps following her and knew Larkin was there. She sighed, stopping at the desk to speak with the nurse, before heading for Lincoln, shutting the door after her. She stood for a moment, hearing raised voices before shaking her head and walking over to the bed, her hand coming out to rest against Lincoln's face. She was tired, she decided, more tired than she could ever remember being. Her eyes were heavy as she watched for signs of awakening or discomfort in his face and seeing none. She finally just crawled up beside him, one arm tucked under her head, the other hand reaching to lay against his face. She knew he could feel her touch, that he welcomed it, and that it calmed him. She prayed for protection for him, for healing, knowing God heard and answered.

She didn't hear the altercation with Larkin that occurred outside the door, with Logan finally drawing his sister away and out of the hospital, Dougal following, a slight grin on his face.

Chapter 10

Lincoln's eyes twitched as he tried to awaken, not sure why he couldn't. He reached for his face, feeling the stubble and wondering at that. His eyes finally cracked open and he slid them shut again, the soft night lights harsh on them. He waited and then opened his eyes, letting them adjust to the light. He stared around, his head twisting to look at the equipment around him, tracing the IV line to his hand. He felt at his face once more, finding the oxygen line there. What did he do, he wondered? And just where was he, other than in a hospital?

He felt the weight on the bed beside him and turned his head cautiously, stopping his movement as he saw the young woman laying there beside him, sound asleep, her arm on his and her hand near his face. That hand came out to touch his cheek as he moved, an unconscious movement in her own sleep. He felt the calming that her touch brought and wondered. He studied her, knowing he knew her, seeing the wedding band on her finger and a matching one on his. He wasn't married, not that he remembered. Sleep claimed him as he tried to puzzle it out.

Four hours later, he was awake again, this time more alert. The woman was gone, he saw right away, and he searched for her, needing answers. He sighed. What had he done? He hurt so much, he knew it had been bad.

Closing his eyes, he tried to concentrate, flashes of pictures flowing through his mind, most of them of the young woman. He heard a whisper of sound and then felt her touch, his face turning into her hand, even as he opened his eyes.

"Lincoln? Oh, my dearest, you are awake. I thought you had been in the night. Let me call for the nurse."

His hand stopped hers as she reached for the call button, and she frowned at him.

"Wait, please. Let me get my thoughts straight." Lincoln shifted in the bed, trying to get comfortable. "We're married, right?"

"We are. I'm Holly. Do you remember who you are?"

He nodded. "I do. Things are fuzzy right now. What happened?"

She began to laugh, drawing a frown from him. "I'm sorry. It's not funny, but I went through this with you just about a year ago. You showed up on my doorstep, not remembering anything about your past other than your name."

"I did, didn't I? Holly? I remember you." His hand reached for hers, clutching tight. "I also remember I have a brother and sister. Where are they?"

"Somewhere around here, I suspect. Logan won't let Larkin near the room. She's been bad, he tells me, and he's right."

Lincoln sighed. "That would be about the size of it. She's very managing, wanting to control. Dad always called her his princess and she's tried to live up to that."

Holly gave a low laugh. "That's what Dougal calls her. I think he's smitten."

"Oh no, not that. They would tear each other apart." He looked away before he looked back. "Holly, what happened? I mean, this time."

"Someone found you and beat you up. No, I didn't get hurt. You made me run."

"That's good. I need out of here. I have to research something." He frowned as her hand kept him still.

"That's not happening, Lincoln. Not until the doctor's been in to see you and released you. You had surgery just a few days ago, to repair some damage the beating did. He won't let you do much for now."

His head back, his eyes closed, Lincoln was frustrated. "Holly, you don't understand. That man gave me a year. It must be close to that now. He's threatened Logan and Larkin if I don't do what he wants."

"It's over a year, by a few days. His men are the ones who attacked you. Logan is aware something was up and he's watching out for Larkin." She fought to keep him still, finally winning that battle, she thought. Lord, please. Don't let him get hurt again. My heart can't take it.

Lincoln finally nodded, conceding he just didn't have the strength to get up and leave. He looked around the hospital room, a frown on his face. "I thought I was in the ICU."

"You were. We had you on a ventilator for a couple of days before they pulled it. Now, you're on oxygen for a few days. Doc said if you kept up the way you were, you can go home on Saturday. That's only two days from now." She watched, concern and love on her face.

"Thank you, my love. I guess I'll have to be patient then." He watched her face, tracing the shadows and fear he could see. "I need to see Logan. And Larkin. I know. She's not been nice, has she?" He watched as she shook her head. "I'm sorry, my love. We've all tried to break her of that habit she has, but it hasn't happened. I know Mom and Dad have spent hours in prayer over her attitude. It will take something drastic, I think, to get her to change." He shifted in the bed, his hand on her arm. "Let her come in. You don't have to stay, but I would like you to."

She nodded. "Let me go find Logan and let him know. He seems to be the only one who has any control over her right now." She grinned suddenly. "Dougal just shakes his head and mutters under his breath. He's frustrated with her and with the situation we're in. He wants it over for us."

"As do we, both of us." He pulled her head down to kiss her. Leaning his forehead against hers, he whispered, "I love you so deeply that I'm afraid."

"I know, my dearest. God has us in the hollow of His hand." She sat on the edge of the bed for a moment, her eyes staring into the distance, not focused on anything. "I had a dream last night, my dearest. God spoke to me. He called you His pilgrim, that He had set you loose to sail the ocean called life, and that He had a safe harbour for you. You had arrived at your harbour, He said. Now, it was up to us to figure out how to keep us both safe."

Lincoln watched her walk away, his thoughts puzzled at her dream. He had always felt like a pilgrim, looking for that place to call his own.

She left the room, with a glance back at Lincoln, before heading out to find Logan. He stood, leaning against the wall outside his brother's room, his eyes on the floor. He looked up, a sober look on his face, as Holly stopped in front of him before she reached to hug him. She felt the shudders of suppressed tears he wouldn't shed.

"Go on in, Logan. He's awake this time. I know you've been in and out. That's fine. Talk to him. He needs to see you." She looked around. "Where's Larkin?"

"I sent her to the motel. Mom and Dad are here. They'll be by later." He looked down at the floor before meeting her eyes once more. "Again, I am so sorry for how she's acted."

"Being sorry is fine. But it's not your actions that are causing the problem. It's hers. She needs to deal with those." She paused, biting at her lip, before she sighed, a shuttered look coming down on her face. "I fear it will take something very drastic to change her. I would not want anyone to go through what Lincoln and I have been through."

Logan nodded, his eyes on the door to the room, not seeing the two men watching from the next doorway. "Thank you for understanding, Holly. She's chased many people away over the years because of that attitude." He shoved away from the wall, his hand reaching out to touch his brother's room door, before his head bowed for a moment. Shoving open the door, he entered, the door swishing closed behind him.

Doc found Holly later in the waiting room, Ted with him. She turned as they approached, a bleak look on her face.

"Holly? What's happened?" Doc reached to hug her, an arm staying around her shoulders.

She shrugged, unable to put into words what she was feeling. Ted watched her closely, before he began to chat about Jake, bringing a semblance of a smile to her face. She looked up as she heard footsteps, meeting the hostile glare from Larkin. She sighed.

"Doc, what is it with her?"

Doc looked up as well. "I can't really say, love. But someone somewhere will deal with her. I just wish it didn't have to be you."

"It will be, I can tell. I have no idea what I did."

"You married Lincoln. That's all you did. You found the love of your life in him and he did in you. You've taken his attention away from her." Doc watched as the older couple moved on past. "Those are his parents. They stopped by to see me. I didn't say anything. I told them it's up to Lincoln and you what you share."

"Thank you, Doc." She sighed again, her heart heavy. "I just wish this was over. I miss my life."

Ted started to laugh, bringing her eyes to him. "That's what you say. You know right well you wanted adventure. I've seen the books you've been reading."

She made a face at him. "Reading them is one thing. Being part of them is something else." She reached to pat his cheek. "Don't you have youth group or something?"

He shook his head. "That was last night. Tonight's a free night for me."

"And you chose to come here. Thank you, Ted." She reached to hug him, hearing a snort from Larkin. "That's it!" She was on her feet and at Larkin before Doc could respond. She grasped the younger woman's arm and all but hauled her down the hallway and into an empty room shutting the door and standing in front of it. "This stops now. There will be no more dirty looks, sly comments, whatever. Lincoln is well aware of what you've been doing. And no, I didn't tell him. I'm sure Logan has told him. So have Dougal and Doc. So lose the attitude with me. Those three men have been friends of mine for years, good friends. I can't say if you've ever had that kind of friendship, but you need to stop with the attitude."

Holly spun and was out of the door before Larkin could even frame a word. She glared at the closing door before she yanked it open and was through it, not seeing Holly. She headed towards Lincoln's room, only to find Dougal in her way, preventing her from reaching it, his finger raised in warning.

"Larkin, you need to stop this. Holly could have you banned from here, you do know that?" As she opened her mouth, his hand went up. "Spare me. You're nothing like your brothers or your parents for that matter. How did you ever end up in that family?" Shooting her a look of pity, he turned and walked away, stopping beside Doc for a moment before he walked past the same two men who had been watching Logan and Holly earlier.

Holly hesitated in the doorway, her eyes first on Lincoln, then on the older couple who stood near his bed. Logan had moved to lean against a wall, his eyes on her as she entered, before he walked towards her, drawing her into a hug with a quiet thank you whispered in her ear.

The older woman turned, then came towards her, stopping short of her as Logan moved aside.

"Mom, this is Holly. Holly, this is our mother, Leigh." He watched carefully, concern in his glance as well as a protective spirit rising within him. He knew at times his mother could come across as harsh. Lord, let this be one time she doesn't. Holly and Lincoln don't need this, not at this point.

Leigh watched as her daughter-in-law stared at her, uncertainty on her face. She drew a deep breath, liking what she saw in the young woman, knowing that Lincoln had given her his heart and that they needed to accept her. She had listened to Larkin the night before and was ready to be hostile towards Holly, but she couldn't. Not when she saw how Lincoln looked for her, his attention not quite on them. She had heard from the nurses their concern when he wouldn't or couldn't relax when she was away from him.

"Holly? Thank you. I have no idea where Lincoln would have been if you had not stepped in." Leigh's hands came down on Holly's shoulders, feeling the relaxation and release of stress that ensued. She drew her into a hug. "Thank you. Both Liam and I are so glad to welcome you into our family."

Holly stumbled over some words, not quite sure afterwards what she had said, but it must have been the right words as Leigh smiled and then Liam walked over to envelope her into a hug.

She stepped back for a moment, overwhelmed, before her eyes went to Lincoln and she almost ran to his arms. His head came down on hers as he whispered his own thank you to her. She leaned back.

"It's okay?" At his nod, she sighed. "I'm glad. Now, I hear tell the doctor will let you go home tomorrow."

"That's what they say. I'm happy with that." He looked over at his parents. "Mom and Dad have asked what they can do."

She looked at him, then over her shoulder at them. "Right now, I can't think of anything. Doc and Martha have been looking after the house for us. Is it safe for them to be here?"

He shrugged. "I have no idea. I would say no, but Dad is adamant they are not leaving, not yet anyway."

She watched his face, seeing the concern he was hiding from his parents as he looked at her. She perched on the side of the bed, leaning back against the upraised head of the bed, her hand automatically reaching to touch his cheek. His mother watched amazed as she saw the calming affect that gesture had on Lincoln.

"How do you do that?" She had approached, standing near the foot, watching the couple.

"Do what?" Holly was puzzled, not sure what she meant.

"You've calmed him, with just a touch. We fought for years when he was tiny to find something that would calm him and never did. Yet, here you are. One touch and you've worked magic."

She stared at Leigh, not quite sure what to say.

Lincoln spoke up. "I'm not sure why, Mom, but her touch is all I need to feel safe and secure. That doesn't make sense." He shook his head, frustrated at not being able to express his thoughts.

"No, actually it does, son." Liam stood at the other side of the bed. "One doctor told us when you were about two that you needed a certain touch, but that none of us had it. She does. Holly, thank you. You've helped him in a way none of us could."

She was embarrassed, he could see, before she spoke. "Nothing special. Doc has said for years I have a way or a touch or a sense to help people. He can't explain it except that it's a gift from God. I hated it."

"Never hate it, Holly." Liam spoke for his wife as well. "When I see and hear what you have done, it truly is a gift from God. Now, about what has been going on?"

173

Holly and Lincoln shared a look. "We're not sure, Dad. All I know is that a year ago I was told to do something, refused, and then ended up here in Cairn. Holly took me in. Whoever it was threatened Logan and Larkin. I still don't know why."

"Then, let us help you think it through. Logan mentioned that you had been back to your office and your home?"

"That is correct. The day I ended up here. We hadn't had a chance to go through much of what we brought back yet." Lincoln's hand tightened on Holly's and she could feel the fear in his grip. "That scares me, Dad, to be perfectly honest. I have no idea what we'll find."

"Let's get you settled at home and then we can research." Liam stepped away as Doc approached, shooing all but Holly from the room.

"Doc?"

He straightened at Holly's question, throwing his stethoscope around his neck. "Yes, Holly? He can still go home tomorrow, but he can't do much. Not for a week or more. We still have to watch for pneumonia with him. And he needs time to completely heal."

"Thanks, Doc. I need to get out of here." Lincoln laid his head back, his eyes closing as he slept.

Holly watched with concern, until Doc touched her shoulder and whispered that she could expect that, given what he had been through. She nodded and watched him walk away, her eyes lifting as she frowned at the man standing outside the door. She didn't know him, but he seemed to be clearly watching her. She walked towards him, and as she did, he left. She hurried to the door but didn't see him. She turned with a frown, her eyes on Lincoln, even as she sensed someone beside her. Leigh stood there, an arm coming around Holly, as she led her back into the room and gently shoved her into a chair.

"Sit, girl. I hear you've been keeping yourself awake to look after Lincoln."

Holly nodded and sighed. "I have been. He needed me to."

"Now, he's sleeping. Let's see you get some rest. I promise. If he needs you, I'll awaken you."

Holly finally laid her head on her arms and did just that. Leigh watched her for a while, before she turned to Lincoln, finding him sleeping as well. She prayed, asking for healing for all of them, knowing there was healing that was desperately needed.

Chapter 11

Nodding at his father in thanks for his help in reaching his home and his bedroom, Lincoln sank gratefully down on his own bed, watching as Holly knelt to remove his shoes, or slippers, he decided. He laid back, grateful to be horizontal once more. He didn't think he had ever been so tired, but then Holly kept reminding him of what he had been through. His father quietly stepped from the room, closing the door behind him, a prayer raising in his heart. He didn't understand the bond the young couple had and guessed he never would.

Holly drew the blankets up around Lincoln's shoulders, then sat beside him, her hand on his cheek. He drew from her strength and calmness, his eyes sliding closed as he slept. Holly yawned, knowing she had guests to attend to, but Lincoln was her first priority. She waited and then finally stood, heading for the shower and clean clothes before she stopped by the bed, assessing how he was sleeping.

Stepping from the room and pulling the door closed behind her, she headed for her kitchen, stopping as she heard an argument going on. She sighed. What was with that girl, she pondered? She's a guest in my house and Lincoln's too, and she just doesn't quit.

Holly turned and walked away, out the front door to sit on her porch, head resting on the high back of the rocker, her eyes closed. She could hear the insects and birds, smell the freshness of the air after the early morning rain. She slept, not seeing Logan coming to find her. He watched for a moment before retreating and then reappearing to sit on the porch swing, his Bible in his hands, his brow drawn down as he concentrated. He looked up briefly as Larkin appeared, saw Holly and then disappeared, shaking his head. This couldn't go on, he thought. They had all tried to reason with her to no avail.

An hour later, Logan looked up as Ted and Dougal approached, Jake running ahead of them, intent on finding his mistress. He licked at her hand, causing her to move it in her sleep to rest her hand on the top of his head. Jake's wise brown eyes studied

Logan, knowing he was a stranger he had yet to meet.

Jake gave a low growl, startling them all. His quick movement awakened Holly, who sat up, disoriented for a moment before she turned, her eyes seeking the trees at the end of the yard. Jake gave a leap towards Logan, who ducked, as Holly screamed Jake's name and for him to halt. Jake was over the back of the swing, hitting the floor behind it, and then over the railing, heading for the trees, intent on whatever it was that had disturbed him.

Dougal gave a shout and then was off the porch, running after Jake. Holly stood for a moment before Logan swept her and Ted into the house, locking the door behind him at Dougal's shouted request. Liam, Leigh and Larkin stared at them, startled, not sure what had just happened but knowing something had.

Holly was away from them, running for the bedroom, her feet slowing to a stop as she drew a deep breath, her hand resting for a moment on the door handle before she turned it and entered the bedroom, her eyes on Lincoln as he still slept. She sank to the floor at the bedside, her hand on his arm, causing him to stir and then awaken.

"Holly? My love, you're here. I dreamt you had left me." Lincoln sat up suddenly, aware of the commotion going on outside. "Holly? What's happening?"

"Jake saw something and took off after it. Dougal then took off after Jake." She gave a giggle, causing him to quirk a brow. "Jake leapt for the swing, right where Logan was sitting, just missing him."

Lincoln grinned. "Now that I would have loved to have seen. What did Dougal find?"

She shrugged. "Logan made us come inside before we could find out." She turned to listen to footsteps heading their way before a tap came to the door. She rose, opening the door to find Dougal standing there.

"Holly? We need to talk." Dougal's face was grim.

"That we do. Give us a couple of minutes and we'll be out." She shut the door, turning to find Lincoln right behind her. "Lincoln, you shouldn't be up."

He shook his head. "It's fine, Holly. I need to be up and around. Let's go hear what he has to say."

She studied him, hugged him and then turned for the door, hesitating as his arms wrapped around her once more.

"I love you, Holly. Never let anyone tell you any different."

She nodded. "And I you. What are we to do, Lincoln? We need you to remember and you can't."

Lincoln leaned against a door frame, his arms around Holly, as he watched Dougal pace, a frown on his face as he then turned to watch his family, sighing as he thought the thunderous look on Larkin's face. Lord, please deal with her. I can't. She just doesn't listen to any one of us.

Dougal's pacing brought him full circle to stand in front of Holly. He searched his friend's face, seeing the fear she was trying to hard to hide, and likely did from those who didn't know her as well as he did. They had been best friends since childhood, and he knew her that well he could see her emotions. At least some of them, he thought.

"What did you find, Dougal?" Holly's voice was low enough that only Lincoln and Dougal heard her.

"A warning carved into a tree, Holly. They have threatened you, if Lincoln refused to do what they want." His eyes raised to Lincoln, seeing the shuttered look on his face. "Have you remembered what it was yet?"

Lincoln shook his head. "No, and I wish I could. I would solve this yesterday if it was possible. I need to go back over my client list and appointments for the year previous to what happened and see if something or a name causes me to remember. But I can't think of any one person who does. The impression I'm getting is that it was someone I didn't know, who approached me when I was leaving work one day, and then it's a blank until I woke up here." His eyes dropped to Holly, who had twisted in his arms to watch his face. "I'm sorry, Dougal. I just don't seem to be able to connect the dots for you."

Dougal just shook his head. "That is what we thought you'd say. We're working on trying to obtain any surveillance tapes that might have been kept, talking to any one around your home and office who might remember seeing someone out of the ordinary, who didn't normally belong there. Gerry's working that angle for us. I want to work with you on your paperwork, if you'll let me."

"That would be fine, Dougal. Tomorrow. Let me get my folks out of here and then we can talk some more." He moved away from Holly, leaving her standing watching him as he went to his parents and then Logan and Larkin, finally persuading them to leave. He swayed for a moment as they walked away and Holly moved to stand with an arm around him, watching him closely.

Dougal headed for the kitchen, and with the ease of an old friend, found food and tea for them. He watched intently as Lincoln sank to a chair, his arm around his abdomen, Holly sliding into a chair beside him, her hand reaching for his face, bringing the calm that he needed.

"Dougal, there's more that you found." Lincoln stared at him.

Dougal sighed. "There is. They've threatened all of your family now, Lincoln." He pulled out his phone, found the photo he wanted and then handed it over.

Holly paled as she saw it, her hand reaching for Lincoln's. "They've said that? Oh my!"

Lincoln read the words, silent anger growing in him. "What does it take to find them, Dougal? They seem to be able to find us easy enough."

"That's the thing, Lincoln. They know who you are and where you are. We don't know who they are."

Lincoln nodded, his eyes on Holly, before a sudden thought hit him. He was on his feet, heading for the office, despite her protests.

"Lincoln? What are you doing?" Holly was on his heels, Dougal following.

"I just had a thought." He stared at the boxes he had gathered from his office. "There has to be a clue in here somewhere." He reached to open one, shaking off her hands. "Let me start, Holly. I can't just sit by and wait."

"I know. What I was going to say is that you have a seat and we will bring the boxes to you."

He finally nodded, turning to sink down onto the couch, his strength suddenly gone. Dougal was watching him carefully and went to Holly, who, at his quiet word, turned to watch Lincoln before she came to sit with him. Dougal moved a table over in front of him, then set the first box.

"Lincoln, we need to pray about this first." Dougal watched as Lincoln nodded, then led them in prayer, asking for guidance, wisdom and a solution.

Lincoln leaned forward, groaning at the pain before Holly moved to stop him.

"You sit back, my dearest. Let us hand you everything." She started to do that, not noticing Dougal rise and head for the kitchen, his eyes on the clock.

She looked up in surprise when she heard Dougal speak and saw the tray he was holding. "Dougal? What have you done?"

"Got us a meal, Holly. I knew you won't. What have you found?"

"This." Lincoln's voice had them turning to him. "I found this. This is not mine. I have no idea how it got into my papers."

Holly took it from him, a frown on her face, as she stared at the photo. "Wait a minute. I know that man."

Dougal wiped his hands and reached for it, his hand hesitating as he saw fear on Holly's face. "Holly?"

"It's him, Dougal. The man I've had nightmares about for years. How does he connect to Lincoln? And just what did he want Lincoln to do?"

Jake whined as he sensed her extreme fear, a paw on her knee before his chin came down on it as well. Her hand rested on his head even as Lincoln reached for her hand.

"You know him, my love? Who is he?"

She couldn't speak, terror driving away that ability. She paled as she tried to compose herself.

"Dougal?" The harshness of Lincoln's voice betrayed his concern and fear.

Dougal looked at Holly before he looked at Lincoln. "He lived here when we were kids. Holly never said what happened but she's terrified of him. No one could get her to say why. He moved away shortly afterwards. His name is Lyle Oakes."

Lincoln frowned. "Lyle Oakes? No, I don't recognize that name." He stood, heading for the desk where he had set his appointment books and then returned to sit beside Holly. "I don't remember anyone by that name." He handed a book to Dougal. "It's okay for you to look through it. I give you that permission and it is part of an investigation."

"Did he have another name?" Dougal studied Holly even as he asked the question.

"I am thinking he did. The initials sound familiar." He searched, his fingers running down the pages before he stopped. "Here. A Lorne Oldman." He looked up. "Can I see the photo again?" He took it, studying it. "It's him. He's changed his hair and put on some weight from this picture, but he's the man who came to see me six months before this all started. He said he wanted a will and other paperwork done, but

I had a bad feeling about him and refused his business."

"And that's why he targeted you. But what did he ask you to do?"

Lincoln tapped at his forehead, trying to remember, before Holly's hand reached for his and stopped its motions. "I wish I could remember. I don't know." The anguish in his voice tore at Holly, bringing tears to her eyes that she blinked away.

"Now that we know his name, we should be able to track him down. Hopefully before he comes at you two again." Dougal stared at his plate of food for a moment, before he set it aside to pull out his notebook. "I will be in touch with Gerry in Hope. You need to let your folks know. Holly, we need to let Doc and your friends know to watch out for him."

"Why don't we just take out an ad in the paper and on the radio? Put his face and name out there." She was disgruntled and it showed.

Lincoln gave a small laugh as he hugged her. "That won't work, my love. It would only drive him underground and we don't want that."

"I know. I was being facetious."

Dougal began to laugh heartily at that. "You? Facetious? Never!"

She made a face at him, then glared at the box in front of her. "Can we leave this until tomorrow? Lincoln needs to be resting."

"That we can. I'm on duty but I'll stop by after I finish." Dougal stood and cleared away the remains of their meal. "Call me if you need me for anything. Got that?"

They both nodded and watched him walk away before Holly stacked the papers and photos neatly on the table and then reached to help Lincoln to his feet, guiding him back to the bedroom. She watched carefully as he laid down.

"I'll be back with your pain medications. Just need to let Jake out for the last time."

Chapter 12

Holly paced the hallway the next morning, listening to the shower running, knowing Lincoln shouldn't be up moving around as much as he was, but powerless to stop him. She sighed. This was too hard, she thought. Maybe they shouldn't have married. Maybe she should have just sent him on his way when he was healed. Not that she could change anything nor would she.

She paused to stroke Jake's head as he sat beside her for a moment. She turned and frowned, heading for the office and the stack of papers they had left there. Her hand shaking, she picked up the photo of the man who had haunted her life for so long. She had wanted to find him and get rid of him as a youngster, realizing as she grew that was no option. She felt Lincoln's arms come around her as he found her, his chin resting on the top of her head.

"What did he do to you, my love? What has scared you so much?"

She began to shake and sobs rose in her throat as she dropped the picture and turned, her arms going around her husband. "I saw him kill someone. Someone he injected something into. A new drug, he said. I was walking home from school and took a shortcut, one I always took. I didn't know he would be there. He saw me and chased after me. I hid, but he didn't leave. He said he would come find me when I least expected it and kill me." She stilled, her mind going back to that day. "But what has that to do with you?" When Lincoln didn't answer, she looked up at him, seeing the grayness of his face. "Lincoln?"

"I remember, Holly. Oh, dear Lord, help me. I remember." His hold on her tightened and she felt the tremors running through him.

"Lincoln, you're scaring me. What did he want?"

"He wanted me to find you and try and buy you off. If that didn't work, then I had to let him know and he would send someone to kill you." Lincoln pulled her to the couch and sank down, not letting go of her. "He wants to kill you, Holly, because of what you saw."

She burrowed against him, her arms tight. "I know he did. I thought he had given up on that when I never said a word."

"Obviously not." He thought through what she had said and knew then what had been asked of him and the devastation he had felt. "It's no wonder I didn't want to remember."

"I know. What would have happened if he had gone to someone else?" When he didn't reply, she looked up at him. "Lincoln?"

"He has done just that, my love. Only we don't know who they are. That scares me. It could be anyone."

"But why threaten your family?"

"He must have thought that if he threatened my family, I would do what he wanted. I couldn't. I don't think I had time to go to them and warn them."

"When you disappeared, he must have thought you had gone to do what he wanted, or else gone somewhere to die." Lincoln stared at her, shocked at her words. "If you had been much longer without treatment or out in the elements, that's what would have happened to you." She sighed. "Now, we have to work to think through this and find out who it is."

"We'll do that. Let's pray hard, my love, that this is over soon. I fear for your life and my family's life."

Holly finally walked away from the couch, turning to watch Lincoln. He had stretched out and was asleep, twitching as he fought against the memories. This time, her touch didn't calm him. That frightened her. She had covered him with a blanket and then sat on the floor beside him, her hand on him, Jake tight to her side.

She headed for the door as she heard a tap at it, peeking through to see Doc and Dougal standing there, Martha beside them. She sighed as she saw the vehicle pulling in as well. Might as well make it old home week, she decided, as she opened the door. Martha took one look at her, swept past the men and hugged her, a whispered prayer echoing in Holly's ears.

"Holly?" Doc's arms were around his wife and Holly as he moved them from the doorway, Dougal instantly alert, going back outside to prowl the yard, Jake at his side, hackles raising. Lincoln's family stood uncertainly in the living room, not sure what was happening, seeing Lincoln stretched out, asleep, before their eyes sought Holly, three pairs worried, one pair hostile.

"Holly?" Doc's voice finally reached through her terror and pain.

"Doc? He remembered." Sobs shook her body even as he reached to draw her into the kitchen and to a chair, Martha's arm still around her.

Leigh followed, Liam behind her, and she reached for the kettle, knowing that a hot drink might help. Logan headed to find Dougal. Larkin shot an angry look at the kitchen before she sank into a chair to watch her brother.

"Holly? What did he remember?" Doc was so concerned, he turned to reach for his bag, thinking he would need to sedate her.

She waved a hand at him. "I don't need your sedatives, Doc. I know that's what you're up to." Her head dropped to her folded arms and sobs once again shook her body.

Liam sat on her other side, a hand on her head, his voice raised in prayer. Gradually her sobs ceased and she sat, her head on her arms, her body still shuddering from the shock of what Liam had said and from her sobs.

"Holly?" Dougal crouched down beside her, Liam moving out of his way. His hand was on her back. "Holly? Come on, sweetheart. What is it?"

She looked up and they all drew deep breaths at the devastation on her face. "He remembered, Dougal. Dear God, please, not that. He remembered."

Dougal studied his friend. "What did he remember, Holly? Tell me."

"He remembered. Dougal, he was to find me and buy me off. If that didn't work, he had to tell that monster who would find someone to kill me. All because of what I saw."

Dougal struggled to keep his emotions in check even as he heard the startled voices around him. Larkin appeared in the door, a frown on her face, not having heard what Holly had said. Holly shoved away and ran from the kitchen, intent on finding Lincoln. She sank to the floor at his side, her arm around him, her face buried against him. His arm reached out to surround her, letting her feel his love and protection even in his sleep.

Dougal moved to where he could watch her, hearing the buzz of conversation behind him, sensing Larkin's hostility beside him.

"Drop the hostility, Larkin. No one has time for your games any more." Dougal didn't look at her as he spoke. When she didn't respond, he turned his head, hardness and anger on his face. "Did you hear what I said? Leave them alone."

"Just who are you to tell me that?"

Dougal's attention had gone back to his lifelong friend and the love of her life. "He remembered, Larkin. He was to be part of a plot to kill her. Now, you tell me. Does that sound like your brother?"

The fierce anger in his voice stopped her words and she stared at him before her eyes moved to her brother, who had awakened and was talking quietly with Holly, his hand cupping her cheek. "No. He wouldn't do something like that."

"That's right. He wouldn't. That knowledge has been hidden deep in him for over a year. That's why he ended up here. Subconsciously he wanted to protect her in any way he could. His refusal to do what the man wanted almost killed him. It may yet." Dougal walked away, moving towards Lincoln and Holly, sinking down in a chair close to them.

"Dougal? You're here?" Lincoln sat up, Holly rising from the floor to sit as close as she could get.

"I am." He watched the couple closely, seeing the devastation in their faces, but the fierce determination underlying it on Lincoln's face and his desire to protect his beloved wife at any cost. "We need to talk, Lincoln. Not right now. Not with everyone here."

"Who's all here?" He looked up, seeing Larkin in the doorway. "My family?"

"Doc and Martha too." Dougal looked down at his hands, not quite sure how to respond to what Holly had said. "Holly said you remembered."

A grim look took over Lincoln's face. "I did, Dougal. I did." His arms tightened around Holly as Jake stood up at his knee, his nose and tongue touching his face.

"Holly said what you had remembered. I'll need as much information as you can give. Then we need to make plans."

"That we do. I would take Holly away from here but he would just follow and we wouldn't have the support that we need." He looked up as he heard footsteps stopping near him.

Liam stood there, his eyes on his son. "No, don't run again, son. We couldn't take it if you disappeared again. Let us help you."

"Right now, Dad, I have no idea what I'm facing or even who I'm facing. You can help by taking Mom and Larkin home and away from here, back to what I hope would be safety. Hire security to be with them until we get this all sorted out."

Liam stood for a moment, digesting the words before he nodded. "I will. There are friends I can call in."

"I know there are, Dad. I have money I can help with that."

Liam's head was shaking before the sentence was finished. "Our friends will not charge us. Not for this." He laid a hand on each of the heads beside him, praying for them, before he turned and walked away, shoulders slumping for a moment.

They could hear Larkin's hushed voice in argument before she stood in front of Lincoln, reaching to hug him before she ran from the room, leaving a sigh coming from her brother at her blatant avoidance of his wife.

Doc and Martha stood for a moment before they approached the three in the living room, Martha sitting near them, Doc assessing Lincoln.

"What caused you to remember, son?" Doc's voice was hushed, as he too sat.

Lincoln shrugged. "I found Holly looking at a picture and when I hugged her felt her terror. She told me what happened when she was so young. That detail was all I needed to remember." He blinked back tears. "If I had been a different type of man, we wouldn't be having this conversation."

"No, we wouldn't. God sent you to protect her." Doc studied his young friend, seeing the ravages of the emotions on her face. "Holly? Can you tell us what happened?" He looked with apology at Dougal, his mouth open to speak when Dougal shook his head, motioning for him to continue, pulling out his ever present pad of paper and pen.

"Holly?" Lincoln voice was soft as he tilted his head to look at her. "Don't shut down on us. We need to get this out into the open and find this man. You will never be safe unless we do."

She sighed, her head nodding against him. "I know, my dearest. It's just that I have buried it so deep."

"We have all day, Holly." Dougal spoke up. "I'm not on duty and even if I was, the chief would tell me to stay with you."

"Thank you, my friend." She looked around. "Where are the others?"

"I sent them home, my love. Dad's taking them home. He'll put security on them." Lincoln thought through what he needed to do. "Dougal, find me someone who can put security on Holly."

"I have already, Lincoln. They were just waiting for me to call and give the go ahead. And it's on both of you." He turned his attention back to Holly.

"Dougal?" Her voice rose in surprise. "When did you do that?"

"A year ago, Holly." He nodded as she gave an exclamation of surprise. "Did you think I would just let you go ahead and live your life without taking steps?"

"I know you wouldn't. I am just surprised you did that so long ago."

"Well, I did." He sounded disgruntled before his voice changed to sternness. "Now, can you tell us exactly what happened?"

She sighed. "I have no choice, now do I?" Her hand tightened on Lincoln's. "Just let me talk, please, Dougal. Then you can ask your questions." She looked up at the ceiling, silently begging God not to have to say anything, then asking, no pleading, for His strength to continue.

"It was when we were six, Dougal, I think, six or seven. I was coming home from school. I always cut through behind the hardware store and through the park there, coming out into the small strand of trees to the road home. It was spring, near May, I think. I heard voices, one raised in argument and then fear, the other deeper, more commanding. The deeper voice was talking about a new drug he had developed, that he wanted the other man to take. The first man was refusing. I crept closer, not sure what I would see. I saw the second man standing over the first man, injecting him with something. The first man convulsed and then laid still. I must have moved or made a noise. The second man stared around and saw him. He chased me until I hid. He threatened to kill me because of what I had seen. He didn't just threaten. He was holding up the syringe. If he had found me, he would have killed me. He finally left and I managed to run home. Mom asked why I was late and I made some excuse. It was horrible, always watching for him to appear. You can't imagine the relief I felt when he moved from town."

"Who was it, Holly?" Dougal's quiet voice finally broke through the silence her words had wrought.

"Lyle Oakes." She looked up at Lincoln. "Lincoln knows him as Lorne Oldman."

"Lyle?" She heard the shock and surprise in Doc's voice. "Lyle?"

"Yes, Doc. Lyle. He hid it well, didn't he? Not one person in town, the good people anyway, would have known him for that, now would they?" She was growing angry, angry at all the years she had lost to fear, about the loss of her father just after that, the loss of her mother, the fear and shadows she and Lincoln had been living under for the last year or so. She was angry at the beatings Lincoln had taken at the man's hands.

Doc sat back, his thoughts muddled before a movement from Martha drew his attention. He frowned before she nodded.

"I had a suspicion, Doc. Nothing concrete. There has always been something about him I didn't like and didn't trust. What could I say?"

"I know, love. I know. He had all of us fooled." He turned to Dougal, who had been making notes and was now watching Holly and Lincoln, a frown on his face. "Dougal?"

Dougal shook his head. "Doc? Lyle Oakes? Lincoln and Holly mentioned his name to me. We're working on trying to find him, but he appears to have gone into hiding. Gerry from Hope is working that town for us, but he's not having any success either. He did say that Oakes had become big in a town past Hope."

"Then, why didn't he go to someone in that town?" Holly was puzzled.

"We'll ask him that when we find him." Dougal tucked his notebook and pen away. "Now, we need to come up with plans for you two."

"Lincoln will be safe if someone is here at the house with him." Holly sighed. "And then there's me."

"And then there's you, my love." Lincoln dropped a kiss on her hair. "We need to keep you safe. And just how do we go about doing that when you're out and about so much?"

"Hire her an assistant. Her business is picking up enough that she could use someone. Find someone in security that could do that."

"Really? Have security with me?"

"It's that or you don't move without me." Lincoln's voice had gotten stern. "I know of a company. They're friends with Dad. There are female operatives working for them. Dad can work it out."

"We can't afford that, Lincoln. No." She was shaking her head. "I can't let you do that."

"It's okay, my love. They won't bill us. I can guarantee you that. They never bill friends for any service they provide."

She finally sighed and then nodded. "Okay. But make sure it's someone who likes to get their hands dirty with mud and whatever it is I get into every day."

"I can do that." Lincoln shared a look with Dougal.

Doc, Martha and Dougal finally took their leave. As he turned from locking the door, Lincoln bowed his head. Lord, this is so hard. Keep my love safe, please, dear Lord? He walked towards the back yard, hearing Jake's bark and Holly's voice. He didn't hear the fun and joy in it that was usual when she was playing with Jake. He stood on the lawn watching for a moment before Jake saw him and ran his way. Holly stood, her arms folded around her.

Lincoln moved towards her, his arms encircling her and pulling her to him. She turned, sobs taking over again. He swept her into his arms and headed for their favourite bench near the back of the yard, sitting, and cradling her close to him.

"Holly?"

"I'm tired, Lincoln. Tired of years of this. When will it ever end?"

"It will end and soon, my love. I will do my best to make that happen."

Chapter 13

A month later, Holly chafed under the restrictions she was placed in. She hated every single moment even though she knew it was done for her protection. She looked up from the plans she was studying, a frown in place, as she watched the labourers working. The garden plot for the city library was coming along, but she knew it was missing something, and that something she just couldn't place.

"It looks good." Hannah, the security agent she had been working with, spoke from beside her. "You have such a wonderful creative talent, Holly."

"It's God given, Hannah. I could not do this." She rolled the plans up and turned to stuff them into the trunk of her car. "It's missing something, and I just don't know what it is. My mind is not on this build, not this time."

"It's understandable." Hannah leaned back against the car, drinking from her water bottle. "You've put in all the plants you can, statues. I know. A fountain."

"A fountain? They would never go for that. It's too expensive."

"What's too expensive?" Hank had appeared at her side.

"A fountain. That's what the garden needs." Hannah pointed to the area. "Right there."

"That's it. That's what I've been thinking." Hank nodded. "Holly, where are your plans for fountains?"

"At home. And no, we can't add. We just under budget now. If we add anything more or have any more delays, it comes out of my pockets." Holly sighed, reaching to tighten her pony tail.

"It doesn't have to, Holly." Hank paced, a thoughtful look on his face. "The downtown business have a fund that you wouldn't know about. At our meeting last night, we decided we wanted to use it somehow here in town but we're sure what. Someone suggested here at the library."

Holly stared at him. "A fountain? Hank!" Her words turned into a plea. "That takes weeks to order."

He shook his head, a grin on his face. "Not if you already have one." He sobered. "You know we lost our daughter when she was little. We had ordered a fountain a couple of years ago to put up in her memory, but didn't have the heart." He pulled out his phone, scrolling to find the picture. "Here. Would this work? I think it would fit right in."

Holly stared at the photo, knowing it was exactly what was needed. "Hank? You can't, but are you sure?"

"I am. Tom, the plumber, will run your lines if you need that. Jimmy the electrician will do the electricity for it." He hugged her, knowing that she hadn't said but would use the fountain. "You'l work it out."

He turned and walked away, leaving Hannah staring after him. "You have such a wonderful caring town, Holly. See what they do for you?"

She nodded, her thoughts on the towns people. "They are, Hannah. I hate that Lyle has touched us in such a horrible way."

Hannah watched her for a moment. "Listen, if you are serious about hiring someone full-time to help you, consider me. I don't want to do security for years. I would like to be like you, find a town, settle down, marry if God wills, raise a family, be part of a community. I like your town. I could see me staying here."

Holly watched her closely, seeing her sincerity. "Then, you're hired. It's seasonal work, but I do work on designs and planning and ordering supplies during the winter."

Hannah reached to hug Holly. "Thank you. Now, we just need to find this guy, get you and your love safe. And oh, yeah, place a fountain."

Holly began to laugh. "And place a fountain. Come on. Let's go talk to Phil and see what he can say."

Holly suddenly shuddered with fear, her feet stopping their forward motion as she stood, before turning to stare around her. Her eyes searched, not seeing anyone but knowing someone was close

"Holly?" Hannah's hand on her arm startled her.

"Someone's out there, Hannah. They're out there and they are watching us." Holly almost ran towards the workmen, causing Phill to frown and walk towards her.

Hannah ran after her, pulling her to a stop. "Holly. Wait. What did you see?"

"I didn't see anyone. Just felt someone watching me." Holly rubbed her hands down her arms and then frowned. "I'm a mess. Let me talk to Phil about the fountain, and then we'll head back to the office, to decide what we do next." She sighed. "I have people out of town who want gardens done. I'm just not sure about travelling."

"If you need to, we can arrange that. One of our guys will drive us. Don's made that commitment to your father-in-law. And to Dougal." She watched carefully for the rest of the time Holly was there before Holly headed towards her.

"Okay. I'm set. Are you?"

"I am, boss. Let's go. Can we stop for food first though?"

Holly stared at her, then at her watch. "Hannah! I'm so sorry! I didn't know it was that time! Why didn't you say something?"

Lincoln looked up as Holly moved towards him through the house, sitting back from his computer before he rose and came to meet her, his arms drawing her close to him.

"How was your day, my love?"

"Busy. Hank offered a fountain for the library project." She rested her head against him. "Hannah wants to hire on full time with me. How was your day?"

"Good, I guess. I have more orders than I know what to do with from the online store. I'm soon going to have to hire out the printing."

"That would be a good idea. You can't keep doing everything."

"No, I can't." He leaned back to watch her face. "But that's not everything, is it?"

She shook her head, her eyes seeking his. "Someone was watching me today, my dearest. We couldn't spot him or her or them, whoever it was."

"I'm sure there are people watching you. We need to be so careful. I know it's hard. You've never had to live like this."

"No, I haven't. Nor have you. Have you heard from your folks?"

"I have. Logan will be here on Saturday, just for a visit. Larkin wants to come but I have told her that unless her attitude towards you changes, she's not welcome."

"Lincoln! You can't do that! She's your sister!"

"She is, but you're my wife. I need to protect you first and foremost."

She finally walked away from him, heading to clean up, knowing she couldn't talk him out of how he felt. She disliked the discord in his family, but knew it was not of her making, and that it would not be up to her to fix it.

Chapter 14

Lincoln walked towards Logan on the Saturday morning, a fine anger running through him. Larkin has not taken the hint, that she should stay away. Logan looked at him and shrugged, apology in the movement.

Larkin moved to hug Lincoln, not sensing his anger, her mind too busy trying to plan how to get Lincoln away from Holly. In her mind, it was Holly's fault that Lincoln had left home and not come back. Lincoln stood, not moving, his anger rising.

"What are you doing here, Larkin?"

She looked up at the harshness of his words. "I came to see you. Logan didn't want to bring me. I made him."

"Larkin, you are not to be around us. Didn't Dad and the security team make that clear to you?"

She pouted. "They said something about that. I don't see any danger."

Lincoln threw his hands into the air. "Let me make something abundantly clear. This is Holly's house. It was hers before we married. It is now our home. You will treat her with respect. Leave your attitude outside the door. If you can't, you will not cross the threshold to our house."

Larkin stepped back. "What do you mean?"

"You know exactly what I mean. You have been intolerably rude to her since you met her and before. It stops now. If it can't, Logan will pack you back into the car and drive away. You will not be welcome around me until such time as you accept the fact that Holly and I are married and I am deeply in love with my wife. Got that?"

Larkin stared at him and then shrugged. "Whatever."

"No, Larkin. No more of that. It's plain and simple. Yes or no. We have enough danger around us we don't need to be distracted by your attitude." Lincoln walked away, leaving Larkin staring after him.

"He's right, Larkin. You have no basis for your feelings or your actions. Do what he says or get back into the car. The choice is yours. I would hate to lose out on a day with my brother and his wife because of you." Logan brushed past her.

Larkin stared after him and then began to pace, not seeing Holly standing on the porch watching her before she too walked into the house.

Larkin paced, knowing her brothers were right, but not sure how to change. She finally turned to the house, her heart breaking at the words her brother had spoken. She had taken very few steps when she saw Holly approaching her, a cup of tea held out for her.

"Larkin? Logan said he didn't stop on the way over. Here. If you're anything like me, you need this."

Larkin studied her for a moment, before reaching for the mug. "Thank you, Holly. Holly, can I talk with you? I need to apologize. Lincoln has made that abundantly clear. He's right."

Holly studied her sister-in-law for a number of moments before she spoke. "Sure. Why don't we head for the back yard? I find it peaceful back there."

Larkin nodded, following Holly as she moved away from her, finally settling down on a bench near the middle of the yard, under a spreading tree. "I like your yard."

"Thank you. My mother planted most of it, she and my Dad. I have just had to do the upkeep, replace plants when needed. I have added a bit. Lincoln has chosen the benches. Mine were wearing out. I think he has good taste." Holly sipped at her tea, waiting for Larkin to speak, knowing that by offering her the cup of tea she had held out an olive branch, so to speak.

"Oh, Holly. What have I done? Both my brothers are angry with me. So is Dad. Mom has tried to talk to me, but I wouldn't listen to her." Tears sparkled in her eyes.

Holly watched with her own eyes narrowed. "Why?"

"Why?" Larkin was puzzled, not expecting that.

Holly nodded. "Yes. Why? Why do things that hurt those who love you?"

Larkin shrugged, her eyes on the ground. "I really don't know. I spoke at length with the minister's wife on

217

Wednesday, trying to sort out just that." She sighed. "I can't really say. It's just, I guess, that Lincoln has always been the one who stood up for me, protected me, made sure I had what I needed and yes, what I wanted. It's hard to share."

"It is hard to share. I was an only child. My parents wanted more but Dad disappeared when I was seven. We have no idea where he went. Mom never declared him dead, said she couldn't do that." Holly leaned back against the bench, her thoughts muddled, trying to sort through what Larkin had asked and what she had said. "Larkin, can I ask you something? You may not know the answer right now, but pray about it and think it over."

"Sure." Larkin turned to watch Holly. "What is it?"

"This is difficult. I am a very private person. Most people know me, but don't know the deep stuff. Dougal and I have been friends since we were kids. We have other friends, but our friendship is a brother and sister type. Do you understand that?" Holly waited until Larkin nodded. "Even Dougal doesn't know a lot of what I have hidden. Your brother is the only one who has ever been able to dig deep enough to find out things. I trust him with my secrets. He trust me with his. We are deeply in love, given what we have been through. Even if we had met under different circumstances, dated and married, I would still have that deep love for him. He also loves God more than he loves me. That is how it should be. Then he loves your parents, you and Logan. He may not say it in words, but it is there. That's why he ran from Hope. He ran to try and find me, a stranger, because he was that concerned. He ran to protect you and Logan. They didn't threaten your parents. They threatened you two. That's what has driven him to stay away. Well, that and the fact he had no memory of you two. I asked him repeatedly to go back, to find you. He refused. His love of you two was deep enough that he didn't want to bring any more danger to you than he had."

Larkin waited, knowing that Holly had paused, but not sure where she was headed with her words.

Holly sipped at her tea. "Larkin. I have no idea why you think I am coming in between you and your brother. As we mature and grow up, our relationships change. At some point, God willing, you will marry as well. You cannot expect your relationship with your brothers to stay the same. I know you feel it is your right to be there when he's hurt, to take care of him. Unfortunately, that is now my place, no longer yours. I am not shutting you out of his life. I welcome you to our lives, to our homes. I pray that at very least we can speak without animosity. If we can't, then Lincoln will choose one of us or the other."

"I know, Holly. I am so sorry. I have been like this all my life, and I can't understand why. Lincoln never told you I was a twin, did he? I lost my younger sister at two years of age. I think since then I have tried hard to hold on to everyone and everything I treasure. The minister's wife helped me to see that and is going to help me work through things."

Holly's mug was on the ground and she had Larkin in her arms in a hug, her tears wetting Larkin's hair. "Oh, Larkin! Does your family know this?"

She shook her head. "I didn't realize it until this week. I need to talk to them."

She hadn't heard Lincoln and Logan approaching, the men stopping as they heard her words.

Holly looked up at the sorrow on Lincoln's face as he sat, reaching for his sister, Logan dropping to his knees in front of her, his arms encircling his siblings. Holly rose and walked away, leaving them to work through this.

"Come on, Jake. We're not needed here right now. Let's see what we have in the kitchen, although I suspect Lincoln has been busy."

She turned later to find Lincoln heading for her, the door swinging closed behind him, before he swept her into his arms, his tears wetting her hair. "Thank you, my love. You reached her when no one else could."

"No, her minister's wife did that."

"That's not what Larkin has said. She said you shared something with her, she won't tell us what, and that made her realize how wrong she has been." He stopped, his emotions keeping him from continuing. "We never knew she why she was like she was. Now we do. It helps us to understand."

"Then, I am glad I was able to help." She looked up at him. "Now, what, Lincoln? We still can't have them stay around us."

"It's really starting to storm. Did you notice that?"

She shook her head, noting for the first time how damp his shirt was. "I didn't. They can't leave tonight, now can they?"

"Sorry, Holly. I had planned on that." Logan appeared in the doorway, shoving Larkin into the room.

"And you didn't come prepared, now did you?" Holly shook her head, loosened herself from Lincoln's hug, and started towards the bedrooms.

"Holly?" Logan's voice stopped her. "We did. We always do." He looked at Lincoln. "Do you have a slicker I can borrow?"

"I do. It's here in the front closet."

Larkin looked apologetically at Holly. "I'm sorry, Holly. This shouldn't have happened."

"But it did, and God has a reason for that. Come on. I'll show you where you can sleep for the night. Then once you're into dry clothes, Lincoln has prepared supper."

"Lincoln? No takeout?"

Holly began to laugh. "No, no takeout. He is actually quite a good cook."

Lincoln stood late that night, watching as Holly slept, Jake stretched out on the floor beside the bed, his eyes on Lincoln. Lincoln's heart was heavy and he didn't know why. He saw the change in his sister, all because of Holly. What was it about her that drew people to her, that led her to know what to say and do that would start healing in them? He had talked to Doc about that one day. Doc had just shrugged, said she had been like all her life, as had her mother, and that sometimes God put people on earth that were needed in a special way. Holly was one of them, he declared, and did Lincoln recognize the treasure he had in his wife? Lincoln had shook his head, replied he did and walked away.

Lord, something is about to happen and I have no idea what. All I know is that I fear greatly for Holly.

Chapter 15

Sunday found the four relaxing in the backyard after their church service. Logan and Lincoln were deep in a discussion of the verses the minister had used. Holly looked at them and then at Larkin, seeing she was not listening to them. She rose, touched Larkin's arm and motioned for her to follow her.

"Holly? Don't you want to stay?" Larkin's voice was hushed.

"No. Lincoln is in his glory, I can tell. He loves to discuss the verses used every Sunday. Usually it's Doc or Dougal he debates with. I can tell he's missed that with Logan."

"I still don't know how you did it over the past year, knowing he couldn't remember, and not knowing what you'd face when he did."

"God gave us the strength, Larkin. Plain and simple." Holly paused at the doorway to look back at her husband. "We've struggled at times, had angry words

225

we've had to ask forgiveness for, doubted, feared, looked for answers in a wrong way. We've been through mental, emotional and physical stuff I would not wish on anyone else."

"But it's not over for you." Larkin took the water bottle Holly held out and then followed her through the house and out to the front yard. The sun sparkled in the sky, sending its rays through the leafy branches to pattern the green grass of the yard.

"No, it's not. It's coming close. That much I can feel. I just wish it was over. He's so afraid for you and Logan. Not your parents. That I can't figure out. He threatened you two." Holly turned to study Larkin. "Now, why would that be?"

Larkin shrugged. "I have no idea. All I know is that I don't like the feeling of being watched, of having to have someone with me wherever I go."

"Like on a date?" Holly grinned at her sister-in-law.

"No. I haven't had a date in a long time. I don't go out just for the sake of going out."

"That's a good policy, you know. Then you don't get a reputation of playing the field." Holly walked down the driveway, heading for the road.

"Holly? Should we be doing this?"

"Doing what?"

"Walking towards the road? Lincoln won't be happy with us."

"Lincoln knows I'll be on the property. We have come to an agreement. He stops hovering over me, I let him in the kitchen."

"And when did he learn to cook like that?"

"He's spent time with Doc's wife, Martha. She's a fantastic cook. He's a quick learner." Holly paused, a frown on her face. "Larkin, did you know Logan's car has a flat tire? We can't get ours out until that's fixed/"

"What? We used it this morning." Larkin's hand suddenly clutched at Holly's arm. "Holly. I don't like this. There should be no reason for a flat tire." She spun, pulling Holly with her. "Come on. Back to the house."

The two women spun on their heels and ran for the house, not hearing the footsteps behind them until Holly was tackled and sent to the ground, the breath knocked out of her lungs, her arms outflung over her head. Larkin turned, heading back for Holly but sliding to a stop as she saw the revolver pointed at her. Her hands in the air, she walked slowly back towards the two men, watching as Holly was hauled to her feet and shoved towards the road and across it towards the trees on the other side. Larkin followed, her hands now bound in front of her, as were Holly's.

Holly desperately sought for a way to escape, seeing none. She wanted Larkin to get away, but how could she? They were shoved deeper and deeper into the woods. She was beginning to panic, knowing they were headed towards the old quarry site. That had been reclaimed by the town and was a wonderful hiking and picnic area. Why would they be taken there?

She drew a breath of relief for a moment as they were shoved down at a picnic table, catching her breath, her bound hands reaching for Larkin. She shook her head at Larkin's questioning look. Larkin slumped back against the table, her eyes on her hands, twisting her wrists to try and escape. She saw furtive movement from Holly and glanced at her quickly, before raising her eyes to the two men, who stood, backs to them, about twenty feet away.

"Larkin? There's a path right behind us. We need to get to it. I know where it leads. We should be able to get away."

"But how? They keep turning around to watch us."

"I know. That's why I want you to go first. Ease yourself around. The path is hidden. It's right behind that maple tree. Go. Now."

Holly watched as Larkin moved and then disappeared before she was on her feet, heading that way as well, disappearing into the trees and finding Larkin, shoving her along the path until she reached a towering pine tree. She grabbed at Larkin's arm, pulling her onto an animal path, carefully moving the brush back into place. She shook her head as Larkin's mouth opened, pointing down the path. She finally stopped, leaning against a rocky wall, her teeth teasing at the rope binding her wrist.

"Holly? Are we safe?"

"For now." She shook the rope loose, then gathering it up, stuck it into a pocket. "Here, I have a knife. I always carry on. Let's get you loose."

Larkin rubbed at her wrists, her eyes first on Holly, then on the path behind them. "How do we get back home?"

"This trail circles around to the road. We can cross it, I hope." Holly set off as fast as she could, knowing that Larkin was tight behind her. She could feel her hand on her back.

Holly slid to a stop, her eyes on the road, frustration evident. Larkin peered around her, a small gasp coming from her.

"How did they get out there so fast?"

"It's not them. There must be at least four of them. Is he that desperate?"

"He must be. Holly, whatever it was, he really wants you."

"And you, too. He's determined to kill me and to use you to get to Lincoln." Holly searched the area before pulling Larkin to the left and along another animal trail.

"Holly? Why?"

"Because I saw him kill someone when I was young. He tried to kill me then. This has festered over the years. He won't give up until either he is dead or I am." She paused, her head turning as she listened, shaking it as Larkin opened her mouth. "Hush. I need to listen."

Larkin stared around, fear on her face. She had never expected something like this when she came with Logan yesterday. Is this what they had been facing, she wondered? Dear Lord, save us. Get us home, please.

Holly finally picked her way carefully forward, eyes watchful, ears listening. She stopped at another trail, this one more worn than the others. "This is a hiking trail. I think it leads back into town. It circles the quarry."

"Circles it? Then how do we use it?"

"We don't. Careful. We cross it to the other path and keep going. Pray hard, Larkin. We are far from safe. That much I know."

Larkin nodded, her hand on Holly's back as Holly took one more look and then ran across the trail, their feet kicking up small puffs of dust, before they were once more hidden from view. They halted, their eyes on one another as they heard voices from behind them, knowing they were from the men searching for them.

"Holly, where to now?"

Holly turned in a circle, her eyes raising to the sky for a moment. "It will be dark in an hour or so. That will help."

"Help? How? We can't see in the dark."

"Nor can they, unless they have night vision gear, and I wouldn't be surprised if they did. They likely have heat sensing cameras as well."

"Oh, great! You're just a bundle of good news!" Larkin grumbled even as she followed Holly.

Holly stopped once more, hearing a sound coming towards her, the sound of men's feet. She desperately searched for an escape, finally shoving Larkin off the trail and following her. She stood, a hand to her throat, the other arm around Larkin, as the footsteps passed them, the loud angry voices echoing through the woods. How would they escape? She spun in a circle, pulling Larkin with her, heading for the road once more, praying they would get across it and back home.

Dark had fallen when they reached the road. Holly hesitated and then hand in hand with Larkin, ran for the other side and the safety of the trees. She heard a sound of a vehicle coming up behind them on the road, and she pulled Larkin to a crouching position, her eyes studying the vehicle. Dougal's, she thought, but she wasn't sure. She wasn't sure about anything any more. She rose, turning to walk away, freezing as she saw the man standing there, a weapon pointed at her head.

"Nice try, lady. Now, turn around and walk back to the road." He raised his phone. "I have them."

Holly felt Larkin moving beside her, not towards the road but off to the side. Holly frowned as she saw the rock in her hand. Larkin, what are you up to? She watched, astounded, as Larkin pitched the rock, hitting the man directly in the forehead and sending him to the ground, to lie still before they both ran past him, towards Holly's home. She knew she was close to it and prayed they would make it without being found once more.

She finally paused in the trees at her side yard, her eyes searching, seeing Dougal and Doc's vehicles, and one she didn't recognize. She heard Larkin give a sigh.

"Larkin?"

"That's Paul's vehicle. My shadow. Why is he here?"

"Because they've been looking for us. Now, come on. Run for the back door. It's closest."

The two women fled across the yard, hearing sounds in the trees behind them, fear lending speed to their feet. Holly hit the door, shoving it open, sliding to a halt as the men in the kitchen turned, some reaching for weapons, Lincoln's face full of fear and then joy and relief as he ran for her, scooping her into his arms. Logan ran for Larkin, his hug tight on his sister.

"Holly? What happened?" Lincoln finally released her enough he could look into her face. "Holly? Where were you two?"

"We had an adventure." Her legs were shaking now, relief at being home. "Lincoln, my dearest. I need to sit. I can't stand any more."

Lincoln sank into a chair shoved towards him, Holly on his knee, his arms tight around her. He looked up as Logan shoved Larkin to a chair near them, handing them both the water Doc had pulled form the fridge.

"Holly? Larkin? What is going on? Where have you two been?" Dougal stood in front of them, arms crossed over his chest, anger simmering under the edge of his words, with fear and concern dancing around the anger.

"We were kidnapped, from the front yard." Larkin finally spoke, her eyes on Holly, wonder in them. "We were taken to the quarry, I think Holly called it. Holly got us away and we made it home."

Holly shook her head. "A little more complicated than that. Dougal, you may find an unconscious man at trail number 5. Larkin has a deadly aim with a rock."

The two women grinned at each other, friendship cemented by what they had been through, the men staring at them and then at each other before Dougal was out the door, backtracking the path they had taken.

Doc approached. "Holly, were you hurt?"

"No, we weren't. Our wrists were bound, but other than scratches from the bush, I think we're in good shape. Check out Larkin, please."

She watched as Doc spoke with Larkin, leaning back on Lincoln, hearing his heart beating under her ear.

"I was so scared, my love, when we came in and you weren't here." Lincoln kissed her.

"I was so worried about you. They are getting desperate, my dearest. To take me from my own yard shows that." She looked up with a frown as the man Larkin had called Paul approached.

"This is Paul. He's with the security team Dad knows. He came looking for

Larkin, having received word they planned to try and kidnap her today."

"Well, they did. They didn't keep her though." She peered around Paul before looking up at him. "How do we keep her safe?"

"In a safe house, I think. We need you to go there too."

Lincoln gave a snort of laughter, causing Paul to frown at him. "That won't happen, Paul. Holly will never go to a safe house."

"He's right. I can't hide. I never have been able to. We need to find him, force him out into the open." She glanced at Larkin and saw her nod. "How do we do that?"

Chapter 16

Ten days later, Lincoln stood for a moment, relaxing against the office door, watching Holly as she worked away. He didn't think she had heard him but when she looked up with a smile, he knew that she had heard him.

"Lincoln? What are you up to?" Holly took at look at her work, and then throwing down her pencil, rose and walked into his arms.

"Looking for my bride. I want to take her out to supper."

"Supper? Is it that time of day already?"

"It is. Come on. We haven't been out to eat for a long time."

She snorted as she walked with him to the front door, waiting as he shut and locked it, Jake whining at being left behind. "Long time? Like a week ago?"

He wrapped an arm around her. "Only a week? It feels a lot longer."

"You know, we don't have many options in town."

"That's okay. As long as you're with me, I'm not fussy." Lincoln tucked her into his car and then walked around to slide into the driver's seat.

"Thank you, Lincoln. Now, the diner or the restaurant or the local fast-food place."

"Let's pick up something and take it to the park. I'm in a mood to eat outside tonight."

"Fastfood it is then." She watched as he parked and then ran back in no time from the restaurant with a sack of food. She reached to take the tray of drinks. "You didn't spill them, running like that. I'm impressed."

"I'll have you know I have great talent at balancing our food." He laughed as she made a face at him before laughing herself.

Seated at a table, they ate slowly, conversation drifting among many topics. Lincoln frowned at the man who walked past them before his attention turned back to Holly.

"Holly? What is going on? You're distracted tonight."

She sighed, her head going down on his shoulder. "I know. It's just that today is the anniversary of when my father disappeared."

"Oh, my love. I'm so sorry. I had forgotten. How can I help?"

"You have, just by being here with me." She raised her head. "Do you think Lyle has moved on? We haven't heard anything. No letters. No photos. No notes. No strangers around the house."

"No, he hasn't. He's making more plans and those plans I fear." He crumpled their garbage into a pile. "I wish this was over. Our lives have been on hold for so long now."

"They have been. Something tells me he's coming close to the end of his plans. That I fear." She looked up as she heard footsteps approaching them and paled. "Lincoln! No!"

Lincoln spun, a blow to his head taking him to the ground, where he lay, a knee into his back, a knife held to his throat.

He could heard Holly's agonized cries and pleas, her voice fading into the distance as she was dragged away from him. He tried to rise, but a blow to the back of the head disoriented him as the world spun around him. He didn't feel the man rise or hear him run away from him. He finally rose to his knees, a hand to the back of his head, searching for Holly and not finding her.

He rose, staggering as he did so, Hank running towards him.

"Lincoln? What's going on? I just saw Holly shoved into a vehicle." Hank's hands helped Lincoln to sit, before he pulled out his phone and called for help.

"He found us, Hank. He took Holly. I need to find her." Lincoln rose and then sat back down abruptly as the world spun once more. "I need to go after them."

"You can't, not with the shape you're in."

Lincoln finally sank back, his eyes searching for Holly, not seeing her. He jumped as a hand touched his shoulder. Doc stood there, a frown on his face.

"Lincoln? Are you okay? Here. Let me see your head." Doc's gentle hands were moving over the back of Lincoln's head even as he spoke. "You've had a nasty blow there. Where's Holly?"

"They took her, Doc. He got her. I need to find her." He struggled against the hands holding him down, looking up in agony as he heard Dougal's voice. "Dougal? I need to get up. I need to find Holly."

"I know you do. Hank gave a description of the vehicle. Tell me what happened." Dougal crouched down in front of him.

"I don't know much. Holly looked up, said something, and then I was on the ground, a knife to my neck. I didn't see them at all." He searched the faces of the men surrounding him. "Where is she?"

"I don't know, Lincoln. I have the details of the vehicle out, the description of the two men Hank saw. I haven't heard anything yet." Dougal stood and moved away as voices came over his radio, turning to watch Lincoln, a grim look on his face.

He walked back towards him. "Lincoln, let me get you home."

Lincoln shook his head, protesting that he needed to stay there, that's where Holly would find him.

Doc finally drew him to his feet, a hand on his back as he directed to Doc's car. "Home, Lincoln. We'll stage the search from there for tonight." Doc shared a look with Dougal, who nodded.

Lincoln paced the house, moving from room to room, his hands reaching to touch something of Holly's, Jake pacing with him, a low whine every once in a while coming from him, his nose nudging Lincoln's hand every few minutes. Doc sat in the kitchen, a mug of cold coffee on the table in front of him, his eyes on his young friend, fatigue weighing him down, a heart raised in prayer. Ted sat beside his father, his head down on his arms, asleep. Doc had told him to go home. Ted had looked at him, shook his head and refused. He needed to be there for his Holly, he stated.

Dougal looked up as the chief approached, beckoning him from the room and to the outdoors. Doc heard a single shocked sound from Dougal and grew afraid. Dougal returned, his face white and grim and sat beside Doc.

"Dougal? There is word?"

"Sorry, Doc. Not about Holly. It was from Lincoln's father. The security agent they had with Larkin was found tonight, barely alive from a bullet wound. Larkin is missing."

"Larkin? Missing?" Doc sat back, shocked, before his eyes sought Lincoln. "How do we tell him?"

"I don't know, Doc. The chief said Liam, Leigh and Logan were put in a safe house. They had tried that last week and they all refused. They had no choice tonight. The police department set it up and they're safe for now."

"Dougal? Any word?" Lincoln sank wearily into a chair, reaching automatically for the cup of coffee Martha handed him. He looked over at Ted. "Doc, you need to take your family home."

"They won't leave, Lincoln. You should know that by now."

He modded, knowing Doc was right. "Dougal? You were saying something about my family."

Dougal stared at his hands for a moment before he looked up at Lincoln. "Your parents and brother are in a safe house. They found Paul tonight, barely alive. Larkin is missing."

Lincoln nodded. "I thought they'd go after her, but I thought she would be safe."

"Why would they take Larkin?" Ted had roused and was listening to the conversation.

"Payback, Ted. I didn't do what he wanted. He takes Holly because that's who he wants and takes Larkin as punishment for me." He dropped his head, and those with him weren't sure if he had fallen asleep, was thinking or even praying. He looked up, a bleak look on his face. "Dougal, what do we do from now on? I know you won't let me investigate, won't even let me move around on my own."

"No, that you can't do. I wish we could have prevented this, Lincoln, but I don't know how we could have." Dougal looked down at his notes. "It's been what five hours, more or less?"

"That it is. I have no idea where she would be taken."

"It will be somewhere around here, I would suspect. This is where it all started. He'll want it to end here." Dougal stood, a hand on Lincoln's shoulder. "I have to run, Lincoln. Call me if you hear anything at all from them." He walked away, his heart heavy for his friends.

Doc finally convinced Lincoln to stretch out. He had a quiet word with Martha and Ted, sending them home, before he settled down in a chair in the living room, a low light on, his eyes closed and his head and heart bowed in prayer.

Lincoln lay still, his heart in turmoil, even as he tried to focus on prayer. He knew God understood when he couldn't frame words, let alone sentences. He just had to cry out. God would hear, of that he was sure. His thoughts tumbled to Holly and he began to weep, softly so as not to disturb Doc, his whole life feeling empty and destroyed. When he thought of Larkin, his sobs began heavier. He didn't hear Doc rise until he felt his hand on his shoulder, and heard his prayers rising for them. He finally calmed enough he could nod at Doc, thanking him silently. Doc rose for a moment, watching as Lincoln drifted off to sleep before he sought his chair and his own rest. Lord, he prayed as sleep claimed him, be with those two young ladies. Bring them home safe and sound, please, dear Lord.

A week went by. Then, a second one passed. Lincoln paced the hall at night, searching through the paths and quarry, anywhere he could think of to find his two ladies. He furiously worked on his photos during the day, trying to keep his mind active and alert, working to while away the time. Dougal was in constant contact as was his father. Doc had the habit of dropping by at odd hours. Ted had declared to his parents that Lincoln needed him and he was there day and night, watching, waiting, serving, following Lincoln as he paced the trails. When he wasn't with Lincoln, he was searching himself, an ear to any hint of where they might be.

Dougal was growing desperate. His heart was heavy that his friend was already dead as was Larkin. That he could not face.

He was determined to bring them home. The chief took pity on him finally, assigning him full time to the investigation with a warning that if he collapsed, he would be pulled off and another officer assigned to it. Dougal had nodded his acknowledge and then left, trying to think of where they would hold the women and coming up with a blank.

Finally, Liam showed up one day, his arms reaching to draw his son into a hug, holding him as they both wept before he stepped back, his hands on Lincoln's shoulders.

"Any word on Holly?"

"Nothing, Dad. Absolutely nothing." He looked up at the ceiling, blinking back tears. "I just want her home."

"I know. Here, let's sit. Tell me everything you can remember of everything that's been gong on. Don's on his way here as well. Where's your writing supplies? In the office?" Liam headed that way, stopping for a moment before he spun. "Lincoln, something different in there. What it is?"

"I don't know what you mean, Dad. Walk through it with me. I've been out back a lot today, trying to take photos."

"All right. Let's pace through this." Liam finally stopped at a section of bookshelves. "Here. What's this?"

Lincoln reached for the photo, his heart stilling as he realized it was one of Holly and himself. "I've never seen this before, Dad." He turned it over, reading the back of it, his mind chilling. "It's from him. He says he has her and she'll never be home." He looked up, fear on his face. "How long has this been here?"

"That I can't answer. Let me see it please." Liam studied it, a frown on his face. "I would say this was a few days before she disappeared. See? In the background? You were at the launching of the fountain at the library? This was taken there."

"That soon to when she disappeared? Oh, Dad! Had we known! But I don't remember us posing for this photo."

"You not likely did, not from the angle." Liam turned, setting the photo carefully on the desk. "Call Dougal. He needs to see this."

Chapter 17

Dougal took the photo handed him, his eyes watching Lincoln's face very carefully. "There has been nothing else?"

Lincoln shook his head. "Not that I am aware of. I can't even tell you how long that has been there."

Dougal frowned. "Then, that's no help." He paced away from Lincoln before he turned. "Lincoln, I need you to search through your house. See if anything else is out of place, been added. You know what I mean. I'll look around outside."

"Dougal, wait. Holly has added stuff to the gardens. I'm not sure you would know what is new or not."

Dougal paused, his thoughts on Lincoln's words before his head dropped. "You're right, Lincoln. I need you to do that." He spun on his heel, watching Lincoln closely. "All right, then. We work together."

The two men searched the house and then the outdoors, not finding anything else.

"This is so bizarre, Dougal. It scares me."

"And me. He's been watching you two, waiting for an opportunity to grab her." Dougal's hand rested briefly on Lincoln's shoulder. "Do you need anything, my friend?"

Lincoln shook his head. "Just Holly." He paused, blinking to clear his eyes. "You know, everyone thinks we never fought. Ted said that. There have been a few nights we didn't sleep, not wanting to until we cleared the air about something. Nothing really major as it turned out. But that was our pact. We went to bed each night at peace with one another. If it was really minor stuff, we gave in. If it was something we felt strongly about, we would argue and go back and forth. We always worked it through."

"I know you did. Holly has that well in her where she drops everything. You've changed that for her, given her someone to argue with and discuss with and work it through. She's never had that, not even with her mother."

Lincoln nodded, his eyes narrowing as he stared out the front window. "Dougal, what is on the hood of your car?"

"What do you mean? What's on the hood of my car?"

Dougal shot a glance out of the window and then was through the door, walking rapidly towards his patrol vehicle, Lincoln at his side. "This wasn't here when we were searching out front. I know that."

"No, it wasn't." Lincoln leaned closer to inspect the package. "It's addressed to me. I guess I need to open it." Dougal's outstretched hand stopped his forward movement.

"Wait, Lincoln. I need to look it over and have the crime scene tech come out."

Lincoln stared at him. "Really? You think it's from him?"

"I would hazard a guess that it is. Doesn't matter. You are not opening it until it's cleared."

Thirty minutes later, Dougal finally looked into the box, shooting a puzzled stare at Lincoln, who moved closer.

"Lincoln, what is this?"

"What's what?" Lincoln stared down into the box, his face paling. "Can we take those out?"

Dougal gently dumped the box out, the rings clinking softly against the cloth he had laid out. "Do you recognize these?"

Lincoln pointed. "That's Larkin's ring. Our parents gave it to her when she graduated high school." Then his breath caught in his throat and he had to swallow hard. "And that's Holly's engagement ring. Her ruby." His voice had softened and then hardened. "What is he meaning by this?"

"He wants you to know he has the two ladies. To send you into terror for their lives. To make a point. To tell you more is coming." Dougal's voice shook before he brought it under control. "He's brutal, Lincoln."

"I know he is. I've felt his brutality first hand." He turned to search the area, his eyes on his home. "How do we find them and bring them home?"

"That's what we are working on. We have had some tips come in, but nothing concrete. That's unusual and very disturbing."

Lincoln leaned back against the car fender, shoving his hands into his pockets. He wanted to pick up the rings but knew he couldn't, that they were now part of the investigation and would be locked away as evidence. "I want those back when I can get them." His chin nodded toward rings.

"We'll get them to you as soon as we can." Dougal watched as the techs searched through the area, shaking their heads at him. "How did he get in here without Jake alerting?"

"That's what I'm wondering. It has to be someone who Jake knows." He sighed. "That's the whole town, now isn't it?"

Dougal gave a grin before he sobered. "That's about the size of it." He turned. "I don't see any tire tracks coming in over mine. That tells me someone walked in and out."

Lincoln finally walked away, around the house to the bench he preferred, slumping down, Jake's head on his knee, a faint whine coming from the collie before a paw was raised and placed over his clasped hands.

"Where is she, Jake? Do you know? Can you show me?"

Jake's bark broke through the air and he stood, a plumy tail swishing back and forth. He turned and walked towards the back of the yard, stopping to watch Jake.

"That way, boy, is it? All right then. Let me get some proper shoes, some supplies and we'll go looking. This time, we won't come back without them."

Ted stood for a moment, watching Lincoln before he spoke. "Not alone, Lincoln."

Lincoln spun, startled at Ted's voice. "What's that, Ted?"

"I said, not alone. I've come prepared to either stay or search. Let me help you."

Lincoln studied the younger man, not a boy any more, who was heading off to college in the fall, and saw the determination in his face. "Okay, then. Where's your pack? We need to take supplies with us."

Ted grinned, holding it up. "All ready to go."

Lincoln shook his head, smothering a grin at Ted's actions, knowing they stemmed from a deep concern about his friend, Holly. He quickly packed what he needed, reached for Jake's leash and attached it, and then headed for the back of the yard.

They searched the paths once more, Lincoln's heart growing heavier with each step. Ted stopped for a moment.

"Lincoln, how far afield have you searched?"

"Probably a five mile radius. Why do you ask?" He turned to watch the younger man, a hand dropping idly to Jake's head.

"Then we need to search further. I have friends who will help. They've offered. We need to go out further, and then further."

"We do. I just don't know how we will."

Ted gave a quick grin as he pulled out his phone, checking to see if he had service. "My friends are waiting for a call. Our teachers are willing to help, using this as a teaching and learning experience." He held up a hand. "They understand the gravity of it, Lincoln. That's not an issue with them."

Lincoln finally shrugged. "Sure. Why not? It's not like I've been able to find them."

Ted walked away, phone to his ear, as he spoke quickly before he pocketed his phone and headed back to them. "They'll be at the picnic area just ahead in about thirty minutes. We plan on searching for a long as we have daylight. It's not just my friends now, Lincoln. Townspeople are coming out. The police chief will be here as well."

Lincoln nodded, unable to speak for a moment because of the tears choking him. "Thank you, Ted. You are a true friend."

Two hours later, Lincoln stood at the top of the quarry, Dougal at his side. He scanned the sky. "We'll need to close up soon, won't we?"

"We will, but they've made good progress tonight. We've been searching randomly. Ted has taken over this and run with it. It's good to see."

"He's a good kid." Lincoln turned as he heard running footsteps, and Ted appeared, excitement in his demeanour.

"Lincoln. Dougal. We think we've found something."

"Where? Show me?" Dougal was hard on Ted's heels as he ran back towards his friends, Lincoln tight on Dougal's heels.

"See? This trail is never used. Not like this." Ted eagerly pointed to the tire tracks they had found.

"You're right, Ted. There have been vehicles coming and going." Dougal reached for his radio, calling in reinforcements. "We're going in to take a look. Ted, I must ask you to stay here. You have found something the rest of us hadn't. Lincoln?"

"I'm coming with you, Dougal, or I'm heading in on my own."

Dougal sighed, knowing he would never keep Lincoln away, not unless he could prove it wasn't a path to the ladies. "I know you are, Lincoln. Stay behind us all. That's all I ask. If you can't, I'll handcuff you to a tree and make you stay. Got that?"

The two men stared at each other before Lincoln gave a clipped nod. "Got that. Now, where does this lead?"

"There's a cabin up ahead. It's been deserted for years. We use it for training at times. Others use it as a rest stop or overnight camping." Lincoln walked slowly towards the cabin, his eyes on the ground, holding a quiet conversation with the chief.

Lincoln followed, not sure where he was heading, but praying that he was heading towards his wife and sister. Lord, it's been a long two weeks or so. Please, let this be them. Please, dear Lord, let us find them and bring them home. Then he heard God gently whisper a question, the question he had avoided thinking about because it was too painful. If they came back to them, only for the family to face a funeral, did he still want them back? Tears clogged his throat and blinded him as he finally acknowledged that yes, he did.

Dougal stopped at the end of the clearing, his eyes probing the area, not seeing anyone outside.

"Chief? What are your thoughts?"

"Someone is here. There's smoke from the chimney. I don't know of anyone who has been using this. They have to clear it with our office before they can."

"I know. That means whoever is here hasn't." Dougal turned to find Lincoln at his side and frowned. "Lincoln?"

Lincoln just shook his head, his eyes on the cabin. "Are they in there?"

"We pray they are and that we can get in and get them."

At the sound of the cabin door suddenly slamming open, the men spun, eyes wide, as they watched a young woman run from the door, hearing cries from within the cabin. Dougal and two of the other officers ran for the cabin as two other officers ran for the young woman.

"Larkin!" The chief could barely hear Lincoln's voice and had to restrain him from running towards his sister.

"Wait. Let my men get her."

Larkin spun, her eyes on the cabin, and she headed back towards it, her cries for Holly sounding through the suddenly hushed clearing. Before she had taken many steps, they saw Holly's form struggling with someone and then the horrible awful sound of an explosion and the rending of timber as the cabin collapsed.

"Holly!" Lincoln tortured cry rang out and he ran towards the cabin, the chief tackling him and taking him down.

"My men are trained, Lincoln. Let them go in."

Lincoln struggled, the chief's words finally sinking in. He sat up, his eyes on the spot where he had seen his wife. "Chief? What happened? Please, dear Lord, let her be alive." He stood and then ran towards his sister, Larkin spinning as she heard him calling for her.

Larkin ran towards him, her arms around his neck as she crashed into him, taking them to the ground. Lincoln sat up, his arms tight around her, tears on his face, sobs shaking both their bodies.

"Oh, thank God. Larkin, you're alive!"

"But Holly! She got me loose and told me to run, that she would right after me. She can't be gone, Lincoln. Please, God, take me instead!" Larkin sobbed against her brother before the chief and an officer drew them to their feet and back to the edge of the clearing.

Lincoln watched as Dougal and the other officers carefully worked around the doorway of the cabin. He heard sounds of running feet and saw paramedics heading that way. His eyes closed and he prayed as he had never prayed before.

Hearing a shout, he looked up and saw a paramedic crawling into the debris, his hands reaching for something or someone.

"We have her!" Dougal's cry rang out as Holly was carefully removed from the debris, a neck collar in place, and then onto a backboard.

Lincoln heart dropped and his eyes closed as he saw the paramedic's head fell forward. No, he cried within him. It can't be. She can't be gone.

"Lincoln. Look!" Larkin's voice intruded on his prayer again and he looked up in time to see the paramedic turn to the chief, a thumb in the air.

"She's alive, Lincoln. He wouldn't do that if she wasn't." The chief's hand on his arm kept him in place. "Stay here. They'll bring her back this way. I can't let you go over there. It's a crime scene."

"I know, chief. I just want to be with her."

Chapter 18

Moving closer, Lincoln watched as they worked desperately on Holly, knowing that she was seriously injured. Larkin wrapped an arm around him, his around her as they watched. She wept quietly, the tears making tracks through the dirt on her face.

Lincoln moved closer as they picked up the basket stretcher, ready to head to where the air ambulance was watching. The men paused for a moment, compassion on their faces, as he touched Holly's face and then bent to kiss her, his hand on her arm as he turned to walk with them. Larkin followed, Ted close to her. He heard the faint whimpers of pain from Holly as the stretcher was jostled. Lincoln knew one of the men had Jake and would return him to their house. His only thought was Holly and her need for a physician and medical treatment.

"Larkin. You go with her." Lincoln's voice was broken as he spoke. He watched as the paramedics moved quickly towards the helicopter that had landed nearby, doors open to receive the patients, the paramedics from the flight taking over their care.

She stopped, staring at him. "No, you should." Her head was shaking as she tried to push Lincoln after Holly.

He shook his head. "You need to be checked out as well. Please? Go with her. Do that for me? I have to call Dad." He watched as the two ladies were loaded in the helicopter and it slowly lifted off and then headed for the hospital. Ted's hand on his arm drew him towards a vehicle.

"In here, Lincoln. They've arranged for transportation for us." Ted pushed him forward before repeating himself, not sure if Lincoln had heard his words. "In here, Lincoln. In this vehicle. They'll get us there as quickly as they can."

Lincoln barely felt the gentle shove into the vehicle. He stared for a moment at the dashboard before he reached for his phone, searching for his father's number, pausing before he dialled, not sure how to tell him that Larkin was fine but that Holly was hurt.

"Dad?" Lincoln heard his father's voice and could almost not speak.

"Lincoln? Son? Do you have news?" There was desperate hope in Liam's voice but caution as well. "Do you have them?"

"I do, Dad. We have them." Lincoln could hear his father relaying the message and then came the sound of weeping, bringing Lincoln's own tears back to the surface.

"Lincoln? Are they alive?" Logan's voice was there in his ear, worried, hopeful.

"They are, Logan. Larkin doesn't seem to be hurt too bad. Holly's hurt. She's hurt bad, Logan." He could not continue.

"We're on our way, Lincoln. God is with us. Gerry's here. He'll bring us. At your hospital there?"

"For now. I'm almost there. Call me when you get closer. I might know more." Lincoln pocketed his phone as the vehicle stopped, not moving for a moment, his eyes sliding closed in prayer.

He finally walked slowly towards the hospital, Ted at his side, the officer behind them, watchful for any danger. He paused at the reception desk and then headed back towards the rooms. Ted waited for a moment and then spun, heading for the outdoors, his phone in his hand as he called for his parents. His father was needed here, he had no doubt of that.

Doc stood for a moment, his eyes on Lincoln, before he moved forward to lay a hand on Lincoln's shoulder, his heart raised in prayer for his young friend.

"What have they said, son?"

Lincoln glanced up, a bleak look on his face. "Not much. They said they had to run a bunch of tests. I can't remember what all they were. That's where she is now." He sank back against the wall, hands jammed into his pockets. "It doesn't look good, Doc. She was in the cabin when it exploded."

Doc froze. "An explosion? Ted didn't say anything about that."

"No? Larkin made it out. Holly was fighting to get out when the cabin came down. I don't know why or who it was she was fighting with. I haven't asked yet." He straightened up as he heard the wheels of the stretcher heading his way, his young wife motionless on it, oxygen and other lines running to her body, a heart monitor in place.

He waited for the nurses to move her to a bed before he approached her, his hand reaching out to touch her face, his other hand reaching for hers. Hers lay limp in his. He studied her face, seeing the thinness of it, the dark shadows, the bruising, the tear tracks through the dirt.

His finger touched her wedding band. He prayed for healing for her, for her to awake. His other hand gently touched her face. He frowned as he stared at her hands before he turned to the physician who had entered.

"What's going on with her hands?"

"She has broken bones in them, Lincoln. We're not sure how or why as yet." He reached for his stethoscope, assessing her, before he stepped around by Lincoln, moving him away as the nurses approached, drawing the curtains around the bed. "Lincoln, over here. We need to talk."

Lincoln nodded, his eyes glued to the curtain, not seeing Doc appear beside him.

"Lincoln, she is remarkably lucky. From what the paramedics said, there was a cavity she was in, protected by the rafters and logs. However, she has suffered a concussion, the extent we don't know yet. Imaging didn't show any skull fractures, which is good. Now, she is battered and bruised. There is no internal bleeding, which we would have expected from what she went through." He paused, watching Lincoln's face closely. "She does have broken bones in her hands and she has a broken upper arm bone. That break is from the cabin coming down."

"Her hands, doctor? What about them?"

"That is what we don't know. I would suspect someone broke them. They are not fresh breaks from today." Lincoln's eyes shot to the physician's and a look of horror came over his face before the physician continued. "Yes, torture, Lincoln. Whoever this is wanted her to hurt." He looked around at Doc, seeing him nod. "I just pray you catch this man. If you don't, she's not safe. The nurses will be through with her shortly and we'll be taking her to surgery to set the bones."

Lincoln paced the waiting room an hour later. Ted watched from his seat, his mother beside him. Doc had left to go back to his practice, promising to be back when he was finished. Lincoln had been in to see Larkin but he couldn't ask her any questions. Dougal had warned him they still needed her statement. He had hugged her long and hard, stating he was glad she was safe and that their family was on their way to them.

Back to the door, Lincoln didn't see his mother hesitate before she was across the room and had him in her arms. He wept as she wept, finally let her draw him to a chair. He felt his father's hand on his head.

"Lincoln? How is she?" Logan crouched down in front of him.

"She's in surgery right now. She has a broken arm." He paused, eyes raised to the ceiling as he fought for control of his emotions. "She has broken bones in her hands, Logan. The physician in Emergency thought it was deliberate."

"Deliberate? Oh, dear Lord, please heal our girl." His mother's prayer whispered to his heart, beginning the healing process.

Lincoln looked up at his parents. "Have you seen Larkin?"

"Just briefly." His father shared a look with his wife. "She was sedated, Lincoln. She hasn't been hurt, other than malnourished."

Lincoln nodded. "Holly's the same. She's dehydrated. Doc talked to the emergency physician. They don't think she ate or drank for the whole time she was gone."

Leigh's arm tightened around her son. "But what are they saying then?"

He shrugged, rising as he saw Doc heading his way. "I have no idea, Mom. They haven't told me yet."

Doc watched closely as Lincoln walked his way before he drew him outside to the hallway. He pointed towards a room. "She's in there, Lincoln. Go on in."

"Doc?"

"They've set the bones, Lincoln. She's got some healing to do." He walked with his young friend towards the room. "She's on IV drips to help rehydrate her. I don't think she has gotten to the point that the dehydration will dramatically affect her."

"But you're not sure?"

"Not until she wakes up. And only the Good Lord knows when that will be."

Lincoln nodded before he shoved open the room door and walked to the bedside, his hands coming out to grip at the bedrail, knuckles whitening as he tightened his grip. He studied Holly's face, seeing the hollows in it, the blackness under her eyes, the chapped and cracked lips. He gently touched the bandages wrapped around her hands, not knowing if even a gentle touch would hurt her. He remembered the surgeon said she would be given pain medications but he had objected to that, knowing how she felt about medications. The surgeon had just shook his head, said they'd give what they could and that Lincoln might need to agreed to something stronger.

His heart broke as he thought of how she had suffered, how much he didn't know and wouldn't until she woke. He drew up a chair, lowering the bedrail until he could lay his hand on her arm and watch her.

A day passed, Lincoln not leaving her side, his family in and out. Larkin found him but still couldn't say much to him. He understood but he still wanted to know. She told him that Holly had tried to protect her and when she was able to get herself loose, she freed Larkin. That's when they had found them.

Lincoln hugged his sister for a long time before sending her with their parents. Logan didn't leave, refused to. Dougal took up a position at Holly's door, only leaving when someone could relieve him. He hadn't said much to Lincoln, but Lincoln could tell they were frustrated. They had searched the rubble but had not found the man Larkin said had been their captor. How he had escaped, they weren't sure. But there had been a blood trail on the river bank but they couldn't be sure it was human or animal until the testing came back. Even then, without his DNA, they could not prove it was him

A week passed. Lincoln was starting to give up hope that Holly would arouse when the nurse came to find him. He had taken a break and was in the waiting room, a cold cup of coffee in his hand.

"Lincoln? Come! Holly is starting to waken."

Lincoln stared at her for a moment and then was on his feet, running for the room, sliding to a halt beside the bed, hope on his face, his hand touching Holly's face.

Holly's head moved restlessly as her eyes flickered, opening and closing without focusing. She moaned slightly as she moved her hands and Lincoln reached out to stop the movement. He didn't see the shadow of the man hovering at the door before he moved on. He felt a sense of danger and looked around, not seeing anyone, before his attention went back to Holly.

"Holly, my love. Come on. Wake up, my love." Lincoln voice held a touch of the tears, hope and fear he had felt over the last three weeks or so.

Holly's eyes finally opened and she stared at the ceiling, disoriented, not knowing where she was, the headache pounding between her temples. She groaned again, Lincoln's hand coming up to touch her face and she flinched, not seeing the pain and worry on his face.

"Holly? Are you with me, my love? Come on. Look at me."

Holly's eyes squeezed shut and she drifted off to sleep again. Lincoln stood, watching, waiting for her to awaken. When she didn't, he dropped back into the chair he had positioned at the bed. This time, he vowed, he was not leaving her.

Chapter 19

Larkin stood for a moment a day later, watching as her brother slept, his head on the bed next to Holly, cradled on his arms. She moved around to stand at the other side, watching the monitors for a moment before glancing at Holly, seeing her eyes were open and clearer.

"Holly?" She kept her voice low.

"Larkin? Where are we?" Holly moved slightly, pain crossing her face as her headache pounded and then eased. She stared at her fingers. "Larkin? What happened?"

"You got loose, untied me and sent me out the door of the cabin. You were behind me when he came in the back door, I think. You didn't make it out before he set off the explosives he had ready." Larkin's hand held Holly's wrist. "They were looking for us and had found the cabin when this all happened." She nodded to Lincoln. "He was there. He thought he had lost you."

Holly's head turned slightly so she could watch Lincoln. "Did they catch him?"

"No, they didn't. They can't think how he escaped. If he was in the cabin, he should have been there where you were. They think he knocked you down and then fled just as the cabin was exploding. They can't understand how he made it out."

"He had a crawl space. He likely ducked down there. He didn't know I heard him talk about it."

"He did? I didn't know that. I don't think the police did either."

"Tell them. It was in the living room area, near the door." Holly paused. "Were you hurt?"

"No. But you have been." Larkin looked over as she heard a sound from Lincoln. "Listen. I need to get back to my room. They're letting me go home today, but I don't want to leave you."

"Go home, Larkin. Be with your family. Stay away from me. I'm too dangerous right now. He'll be coming back for me as soon as he knows I didn't die. That was his aim. He really didn't care if you made it out or not. That was just icing on the cake for him if you didn't." Holly turned towards Lincoln as she felt his hand on her face. "Lincoln? You're awake."

"As are you." Larkin gave Holly's arm a squeeze, stopped to drop a kiss on her brother's cheek and then headed out of the room, gently shutting the door behind her.

"Holly?" Lincoln's voice was cautious. He was not sure if Holly was really awake.

"Yes, my dearest, I'm awake. At least, I think I am. But for how long I don't know." Her eyelids flickered up and down as she fought to stay awake. "I'm sorry. I just can't keep my eyes open."

"Then, sleep, my love."

She shook her head, grimacing with pain. "I don't want to, Lincoln. The dreams are there and I can't get away." Her eyes opened and sought reassurance from him. "Don't let him get Larkin again. He'll kill her, just to spite you."

"I know he will. He tried." Lincoln rested an elbow on the bed and propped up his chin on his hand. "I'm so thankful you're here."

She looked past him. "Dougal? You're here. For my statement I suppose."

"If you're up to it, we do need to get one."

She sighed. "I can give it. It's not easy though. I may fall asleep part way through and then you'll have to come back."

Lincoln gave Dougal a hard look. "Make it quick."

Dougal shook his head. "I'll make it as quick as I can. We have Larkin's statement."

"Okay, you two. Enough. If you don't stop, I'll put you out of the room and post a sign that you're not allowed." She motioned for her water and Lincoln held the cup to her mouth. "Okay, where do I start?"

Lincoln reached for her hand, a frown on his face. "Only if you're up to it, my love."

She shook her head, grimacing at the pain. "I need to, Lincoln. They need to find him. If they don't I won't survive." She looked at Dougal. "Do you have your dictator? I can't write." She held up her hands. "I can explain these as well."

Dougal was prepared and pulled his dictator out of his briefcase and set it ready to go. "Just say when you're ready."

She nodded. "All set."

She started with her name, the date and where she was. She paused, gathering her thoughts, Lincoln's hand on hers, careful of the splints and bandages.

"It started when Lincoln and I were just finishing our meal that night. I don't think Lincoln saw the men coming towards us. They were there before I could warn him. They forced me into a vehicle and I hit my head, I think, or they drugged me. I can't really remember which it was. When I awoke, I was in a shed or garage. From there, about two days later, I was taken to the cabin. Larkin was already there. I had no idea they had taken her.

"We were there for what seemed forever. Lyle would come and go, always leaving one of his men to watch us. We were tied up, but one day I managed to get loose and had Larkin almost loose when they came back. He shoved me and I fell.

With the way I fell, that's when I broke the three fingers. No, four, I guess. He refused to let Larkin do anything with them. He made sure I couldn't get loose again.

"He taunted us, telling us that Lincoln was already dead. That Larkin's family had been punished. That he had hurt people close to me. He played mind games with us."

She paused at that point, Lincoln handing her the glass of water and she drank deeply. "After two weeks, he changed. He became more belligerent towards us. Never physical. He never touched us after that one day he pushed me. He would bring out his syringes and vials of drugs and threaten to inject us, telling us that we would be hooked on them or else they would kill us. He never did inject us.

"I refused to eat or drink. I didn't trust that he would not put something in our food. Mine, anyway. I think he wanted to keep Larkin alive long enough to have her see Lincoln dead. That's what I overheard him say one day. It scared me. I tried to hard after that to get away.

"I think that conversation was about a week before we escaped. He didn't know I could hear him, but his voice was really loud. He was talking outside to someone I didn't know. It would seem the person was not his employee. It was more like he was doing what that person said. That doesn't make sense, not from what I can remember." She shrugged at that point, her eyes on Dougal, who was watching her closely and taking notes.

"That last day, I worked on my bonds. They hadn't been tied back as tight. I was able to get free, found a knife and freed Larkin, sending her out the door. Just as I was heading there, he tackled me. We struggled and then I heard him exclaim something. He turned, pulled up a trap door, and was gone. Before I could get to my feet, I heard an explosion. I don't remember anything after that." Terror shone on her face for a few moments. "Before he found me, I found some papers. I tucked them into a pocket. He had been looked at them that morning and muttering to himself."

She looked up at Lincoln, finding his eyes steady on her. "I can't think of anything else."

Dougal shut off the dictator, his eyes on her as she settled back and drifted off to sleep before he spoke. "She knows more than she's saying, Lincoln."

"I know she does. She's hiding what she knows because she thinks I'll go after that monster."

"I'm sure you want to. Leave it to us. We didn't know about the trap door. In all those years we've been using it, no one ever mentioned it." Dougal studied his notes. "We'll need those papers."

"You may find it a recent addition. He's been using the cabin as a base, I would imagine. He's from here so he would know about it." She shared a look with Lincoln. "I have no idea what happened to the papers." Holly had roused once more, spoken briefly and then closed her eyes

"That he would." Dougal picked up the dictator, dropping it into his briefcase and then snapping the case closed. "I'll have this transcribed and then bring it back." He paused, his eyes on Holly. "Keep her safe, Lincoln. We have an officer at the door but this man has proven he can get to you two without much trouble."

"I know he can. Make sure my family stays as far away from us as they can. For now, at least. Paul's on the road to recovery but I don't want anyone else hurt. Not if I can help it. I'll get those papers to you later. I had Dad lock them away."

Dougal stared at him, his eyes narrowed. "Just what are you thinking?"

Lincoln shook his head. "I'm not saying for now. I have an idea of how to catch him, and will need your help but I need to refine my plans." Lincoln rose, hand outstretched to shake Dougal's. "Dougal, you have been with us through so much. You've been a friend to Holly for years. Thank you."

Dougal didn't say anything, just nodded as he walked away, his mind already trying to think through what Lincoln might have planned before he shook his head. He had no idea what Lincoln would be planning.

Holly had drifted off again as the men were discussing the situation. She didn't see Lincoln watching her before he walked out the door, to find his father. They spoke for a few moments before Lincoln headed back towards Holly, nodding to the security personnel stationed outside her door. Liam's friend had pulled in his men, offering them to the chief, who had gratefully accepted their aid.

Lincoln slouched back in the chair, his eyes on Holly, his thoughts on what she had said and the horror the two ladies must have endured. He was horrified at what they had gone through and was determined to find the man and bring him to justice. He reached for Holly's hand, holding it tight, not wanting to let her go, not when she was back to him.

Doc stood for a moment, watching his friends, before he walked towards Lincoln and then began his assessment of Holly.

"Doc?" Lincoln voice, though low, roused Holly.

"Doc?" Holly's voice brought their attention to her. "When can I go home?"

Doc studied the IV and then the monitors. "I think by tomorrow we can let you go home." He heard her sigh of relief. "There are restrictions on you. At least for a few weeks." He nodded towards her fingers. "Those splints are on for four

286

weeks at the minimum. That means you can't be digging in the dirt."

She nodded. "I know. I figured that is what you would say." She saw the dark look on his face. "I fell on my hands, Doc. That's how they broke. He didn't do that to me. He was very careful, for some reason." She paused, her thoughts muddled. "That's strange. He made sure he didn't hurt us. He'd threaten us but other than that, he kept away from us. Other than when he tried to keep me from escaping."

Doc watched her closely, knowing her well enough to understand she was hiding something, something she wasn't ready to tell him. He prayed for her healing, for her trust in them to be restored. He wasn't quite sure what all was going on with her but he feared for the young couple. He knew until Lyle and his men were captured, they would not be free to live their lives. They had been under this shadow as a couple for over a year. For Holly it had been most of her life. He flipped open her chart, studying the blood work and then an ultrasound, his eyes raising to watch the two as they talked quietly. He sighed, knowing that was not the time to go over those particular results.

He didn't think either were ready. Then he paused. No, it was not right. As a physician he had to tell them.

"Doc?" Holly's quiet voice reached through his thoughts and he smiled at her.

"Yes, Holly?"

"Why the frown?" She tilted her head to watch him. "There's something wrong, isn't there?"

He shook his head, his eyes on Lincoln as Lincoln in turned watched Holly. "No. There's not. You're going home tomorrow. Late today if the blood work comes back good." He paused, opening the chart again. "I'll leave instructions with the nurses for you."

Thirty minutes later, the nurse was in the room, pulling the IV, and smiling happily at Holly. "Doc's cleared you to go home."

"Oh, how wonderful! Now if I can get dressed, I'll be gone."

Shortly after, Lincoln settled her into a wheel chair, their security team surrounding them, as the nurse approached, Holly's paperwork in her hand, a sealed manilla envelope on top.

"What is this?" Holly touched the envelope.

"I have no idea. Doc left it this morning, said to give it to you when you left. He didn't say what it was."

Jake was beside himself with happiness, barking, whining, jumping up to lick at Holly's arms and then face. She laughingly pushed him away and pointed to the living room. Lincoln started to shake his head and then grinned.

"Sure, why not?" He settled her on the couch and headed for the kitchen, knowing Martha had been there. "What do you feel like to eat?"

"Toast maybe. A good cup of tea. The tea in the hospital is so bitter." Holly's arms wrapped around Jake, her eyes on the envelope. "What do you think Doc has sealed up in that envelope?"

Lincoln appeared shortly, a tray in his hands, before he tucked pillows and a blanket around her, a prayer of thankfulness raising from his heart. He settled himself beside her, his mug of coffee in his hand, watching as she nibbled at her food.

"It's going to take you a while to eat well."

"I know. I will never look at food the same again. That much I know." She reached for the envelope, turning it over and over in her hands before thrusting it at him. "I can't open it. I'm scared, Lincoln, that it's bad news. I can't take any more bad news."

His mug on the table, his arm around her, he took the envelope and turned it over and over. He felt her head come down on his shoulder and her body relax against him as she slept. He set the envelope to one side and just sat, watching his wife.

Chapter 20

Three days later, Holly stared at the envelope still sitting on the table in the living room. Neither one of them had made an effort to pick it up again or open it. She sighed. Lord, we're avoiding it, aren't we? She knew Lincoln was out and about, his camera in his hand. They both wanted to get away, to travel somewhere they didn't know anyone and just be together, somewhere they could enjoy nature, where he could take his photos and she could see inspiration for her work. That wouldn't happen until Lyle was caught, she thought.

She reached for the envelope, taking it to the office and setting it on her desk, before she sat in her chair, her eyes on the envelope and finally ignoring it, she turned to her computer. She placed her hands on the keyboard and then frowned before she gave a thankful prayer that she was still alive and able to type.

Lincoln found her later and dropped a kiss on her cheek before sitting in the chair across from her.

"Working hard?"

"I'm trying to. I have so much to catch up on." She blew out a breath of frustration, before her eyes raised to him. "We're avoiding that, you know."

"I know. I don't think either one of us wants to be the one to find out bad news." He poked at the envelope before she moved it, sticking it into a drawer. "Hiding it won't make it go away, you know."

"I know. I just can't deal with that right now. I have no idea what Doc was up to. He's been quiet, and that's not like him." She raised her eyes to the ceiling, praying for her friends. "Lincoln, what are we being taught with all this?"

"Being taught? Patience, trust, peace." He looked down. "It was so hard when you were gone. I didn't sleep much, didn't eat much. All I could do was pray for you to come home." He paused, not sure how to continue. "I had come to the point that morning, the day you were found? I had come to the point I had to surrender both you and Larkin to God. To tell Him that if you didn't come home, if you came home and were changed, if you came home and we had to bury one or both of you, that I understood. That I understood you were in His hands and He had ultimate control over what happened."

Holly had been watching him closely, knowing what he was saying. "I think I had come to the same conclusion, Lincoln. I didn't know if we would survive. I had to leave it with God. That's all I could do. I had tried to escape but hadn't made it out." She sighed, blinking back tears for a moment. "It's hard, you know? Hard to realize that we're both free and home with our loved ones, but we're still not free. We won't be free until he is caught. Dougal can't say when that will happen. They can't find him."

"Dougal said they found the trap door. It led to the drop-off behind the cabin. It's new, from what they can determine. He must have dug that. It opened out into a depression there." Lincoln rose and began to pace. "I want this over, Holly. It's been hanging over you for so long. It's dictated your life. You need to be free of that." He sighed, sorrow on his face. "And then there's us. You have never known true freedom."

Holly rose, moving towards him, her arms around him. "I will never regret meeting you or having you in my life, my dearest. You have helped me to come to terms with what happened. Your faith in God has led me to a deeper faith."

He hugged her tight, his face buried against her. They stood for how long, they were never sure before Holly moved away, her eyes on the outside. "Jake's found something. What is it he has?"

Lincoln was out the door and back in no time, a frown his face. "It looks as if our friend has been around."

Holly paled. "No, it can't be. Can't he just leave us alone?"

Lincoln's arms were around her and he was leading her to a seat. He gently shoved her down, his eyes on the package he was holding. "He's not done, my love. He's toying with us."

He set the package to one side, pulling out his phone. "Dougal? He's sent a package. Can you come get it? I have not opened it and I won't. Jake found it."

Dougal stood over the package an hour later, a puzzled frown on his face. "I don't think this is from him."

"What do you mean?" Holly moved closer, peering into the box. "Oh, my! I don't think it is either. That's my Mom when she was younger, around the time she and Dad married." She looked up at Lincoln, fear on her face. "What does this mean?"

"I have no idea, Holly, but we will look into this." Dougal sealed the package into an evidence bag. "And how are you feeling?"

"I was feeling better until I saw that."

Lincoln wrapped Holly in his arms, her arms wrapping around his, his chin resting on her shoulder. "Dougal, are you any closer to finding him?"

Dougal stared at the bag he was holding before he shook his head. "I'm sorry, Lincoln. We're not. I have no idea where we're going from here. He's vanished into thin air again."

"He can't have. Have you been back to the cabin?" Holly looked up, a shadowed, shuttered look on her face. "He'll go back there. You won't expect him to."

"We've had men in and out of there over the last few days. There has been no sign of him."

Holly shrugged. "He has to be. There has to be another area there he's hiding in. That's the only explanation."

Dougal nodded then headed for the door. "Stay away from that area, Holly. It's too dangerous right now."

Holly didn't respond but Lincoln felt her body tense.

"Holly? What are you thinking?"

"I'm thinking that I need to go there. I need to face where I was held." She turned in his arms, her hands coming up to rest on his upper arms as she leaned back to look up at him. "Does that make sense?"

"It does, my love. And we will do just that."

"Lincoln? Are you sure?"

He nodded. "We need to, both of us. We need to face that, and God willing, put it to rest." He hugged her tighter, knowing they both still faced danger. "Dad's got everyone there tucked away. This is hard on them. They don't understand just how dangerous it is."

"Did Don pull his men?"

"He said he wasn't going to but I haven't seen them today. And I don't like that. He would have told me if he was leaving us alone."

"I know." She moved away from him, intent on looking out the window when Jake moved in front of her. "Jake? What is going on?"

Jake gave a low woof and then headed for the door, his tail sweeping back and forth. Once he was outside, he disappeared towards the trees at the side. Lincoln frowned and then followed, Holly tight to his side, her hand in his.

"Lincoln, what has he found? It can't be bad. He's acting like he's found a friend."

Lincoln stopped suddenly, his eyes on the older man who had crouched down and was loving on Jake, who was in turn leaning hard on him.

"Excuse me?" Lincoln stood between Holly and the man, his eyes narrowed. As the man looked up, he frowned. The man looked familiar but he didn't think he had ever met him.

The man stood, his clothes worn and faded. He had a graying beard covering a face lined with care and worry and just life in general. He walked slowly towards the couple, hands in the air.

Holly studied him, then moved to stand beside Lincoln, her hand reaching for his.

"I know you, don't I? You're the man who helped me get away before." She watched as he nodded. "But I know you better than that."

The man's throat worked as he swallowed, his voice not working. He nodded. "You do, Holly." His voice was rough with emotion

Holly frowned again. "Where do I know you from?" Releasing Lincoln's hand, she walked towards the man, Lincoln on her heels, Jake standing by the man, his eyes on his mistress, his tail wagging slowly back and forth.

"You know me well, Holly. It's been many years. Far too many years." They heard the tears choke off his voice.

Holly stopped short on him, her eyes studying him before she gave an exclamation of first dismay, then joy. Lincoln's hands were on her shoulders and he felt her shudder.

"Holly? What's going on?" His voice was low in her ear.

"Dad? Is that you? I thought you were dead." Tears blinded her and she reached to touch Lincoln's hands.

"It is, Holly. It's a long story. I was imprisoned overseas." He looked around. "Can we go inside somewhere? It's not safe for you to be out here."

Lincoln turned, pointing to the house. "In there. It's getting dark, so let us go ahead. You slip up after it turns dark, to the back door. We'll leave it unlocked, but the lights will be off. You're familiar with the house?"

"I should be. I helped my Dad build it." He watched his daughter's face. "Go on, Holly. Go in where it's safe. I'll be in shortly." He stepped back into the trees, disappearing from their view.

Lincoln drew Holly away and back to the house, Jake pacing beside her.

"My Dad? After all these years?" She was in shock, worrying at the bandages on her splinted fingers until Lincoln's hands stopped her.

"He'll explain. Here. Sit. You're getting tired, I know." He gently seated her, reached for the kettle and made her a tea, setting it and a sandwich in front of her. "Eat, my love. You need your strength."

She nibbled at her food, her eyes on the door, watching as dusk set in, waiting for her father to appear.

"Holly?" Lincoln sat beside her, his hands reached for hers. "I know it's been a long time. Let him speak. I don't think he stayed away on his own."

They both started as the door opened and the man slipped inside, Jake rising to meet him, his tail wagging as he welcomed a friend.

Chapter 21

Lincoln rose to stand behind Holly, his hands on her shoulders as she watched the man closely before she relaxed, her hands reaching for his. Frustration was evident as she pulled them back to stare at the splints.

Lincoln moved towards the man, his head tilted to one side as he studied him. He spoke quietly to Jake who moved away to stand beside Holly, his head lowered so he could watch the two men from under the table.

Holly rose, walking towards her father, her hands reaching out for his. He hesitated, not sure if he should be touching her before he swept her into his arms, tightening his hold on her as he wept. Holly's tears soaked his shirt. How long they stood there, afterwards they were never sure before Lincoln's arms came around the two of them and then he gradually moved them to the living room. He left and returned with the tray of food and coffee and tea he had prepared, setting in on the coffee table before he sat beside it.

Holly held her father's hand, her eyes on him before she turned to Lincoln. He smiled gently at her and nodded. He could see the resemblance. He sighed. This was something he needed to investigate but not now.

"Holly? You are okay? I tried to find you when you disappeared but he had hidden you too well."

Her father's gentle touch had the tears back in her eyes and she blinked rapidly to clear them away. "I am, Dad. But you? What happened? Mom never gave up hope you'd come home." Her free hand went to her mouth and she stopped speaking. "Mom! You know?"

"I heard and then I went to the gravesite. I am so sorry, my girl. I tried to get away but just couldn't. Someone finally found me and freed me. I'm not sure who it was but they said Doc had finally found me and paid them to get me out and back here."

"Doc? So that's what he's been up to. I knew he had been up to something."

"He was a good friend when we were younger. It sounds as if he's been a good friend to you."

"He has been, Dad." She shared a look with Lincoln. "But what happened?"

He sighed. "It's not a pretty story, my girl." He nodded his thanks as he took the cup of coffee Lincoln held out to him. "You were, what six or seven, when I had to travel overseas. I didn't want to go. I think I sensed something was off about that trip. I had to go for my employer, searching for contacts for the imports that he offered. I hear he's no longer in business. That when I disappeared his business failed, through no fault of his own. He was a good boss, honest and reliable. Anyway, when I reached that country and I won't say which one, I was arrested just after I arrived. Something about smuggling. I knew it was a false charge but I was whisked away and imprisoned without a trial or even being able to contact your mother or the embassy. When someone appeared some months ago, whisked me away to another country, I had hope that I might finally be free. It took some time to get back here." He paused to sip at his coffee, trying to control his emotions. Lincoln had moved to sit beside Holly, his arms tight around her. Jake sat with his chin on the man's knee.

"Anyway, I eventually made it back here. I've been living outside of town, having heard that your Mom was gone, Holly, and that you were in trouble. That someone was trying to kill you and your young man here." At that point, he looked up at Lincoln and Lincoln saw the similar eyes to Holly's. "Thank you for doing what you've been doing to keep her safe." He gave a small smile. "And yes, I have heard your story. Something right out of those books your Mom used to read you at bedtime, my girl."

"I know, Dad. I am just so glad you're here. But where do we go from here?"

Lincoln looked around as he heard a soft tap at the door. "Stay put."

He stared as Doc stood on the porch for a moment before moving towards Lincoln, making him step back. "Doc?"

"It's okay, Lincoln. I know he's here. He got word to me." Doc moved past him into the softly-lit living room, his eyes first on Holly and then on her father as he stood, a smile on his face as he stretched out a hand to greet an old friend.

Doc stood back finally, his eyes on Holly. "I couldn't tell you, Holly. He said I couldn't."

"That's what you've been up to. Well, at one of your tasks." Holly hugged Doc, and then hugged her father. "I'm just so glad you did. It was the area code of the call, wasn't it, Doc?"

"It was. That set off a search. I found someone who could go in and get him out of the prison and to another country. It took some work. I couldn't and wouldn't tell you." He turned to his friend. "Callum, I can't tell you how sorry I am it took this long. Martha and I have searched this country. I didn't realize you would be overseas."

"Thank you, Doc. You succeeded. I just wish it had never happened, but God is in control. I was able to witness for Him in that prison, as brutal as it was at times." He paused, his thoughts on what he had faced, before he looked up at Lincoln. "And you, young man, you have proved your sterling worth in how you have stepped in with my girl. I can never thank you enough."

Lincoln shrugged. "I love her more than my own life. I will do whatever it takes to keep her safe."

Callum nodded, before he sat back down, exhausted. "This takes so much from me. I'm still not back to my full strength."

Lincoln watched at Holly sat beside her father, Doc hovering over him before he spoke.

"Who was it, Callum? Who put you in prison over there? If I had to guess, I would say Lyle."

Callum looked up sharply at that before nodding. "And your guess would be right. He visited me a few times, always taunting me. He wanted me to respond and then the punishment would have increased. I never did. God restrained me." He paused, wonder on his face. "God sent a dream the night before your men got to me, Doc. He came to me, told me I was leaving that place and that I would see my girl again. I think I knew then that my Lizzie was gone." He stopped, overcome with emotion for a moment before resolve took over. "Now, how do we get to Lyle? I heard tell he's gone underground."

"He has. We're trying to find him but have been unable to so far."

Callum nodded, his eyes on Lincoln, whose own eyes had narrowed at a thought. "Lincoln, whatever it is you're thinking, don't do it. Don't put yourself out there as a target. If it comes to that, I'll be the one."

"I won't unless I have to." Lincoln paced. "Now that you're here, we need to make plans." He sighed as he stopped, his head going back. "We have to bring in Dougal."

"We will. Not tonight." Doc shook his head. "It's enough that we have Callum here." He looked around. "Holly, pens. Paper. Let's make some plans."

She ran for the office, returning with what he asked for. Various situations and scenarios were tossed around before the plans began to come together. Lincoln listened to the two men, letting them lead, speaking up when he felt he had to.

Doc finally stood, his eyes thoughtful as he watched, before they closed and he prayed, knowing that a crisis was coming and they were helpless to prevent that. Only

God could step in and somehow, Doc wasn't sure if he would.

Lincoln settled Callum in one of their spare rooms before finding Holly in the kitchen, a low light on, clearing away the remnants of their meals. He swept her into a tight hug, feeling her arms tighten around him.

"Are you okay?" He felt her shrug.

"At this point, my dearest, I have no idea. My emotions are just so mixed." Her hand came to his face and he leaned into it. "I sense your emotions are just as mixed."

"They are. I fear for us, my love. I know he's coming for us and I'm helpless to prevent just that."

"I feel the same way." She paused, her eyes studying the face she loved. "I knew Doc was up to something."

"He's a good friend. I'm glad he's been here for you."

"For us." She turned, looking around the kitchen. "It looks as if we're set for the night. Jake, come. Time for bed."

Chapter 22

A day later, Holly turned from her job site, seeing her security personnel as he told her to call him, waiting by his vehicle, his eyes not on her but on the surrounding area. She knew there would be another vehicle somewhere close, with that person also on watch. She hated this. She hated losing her freedom but understood the need for this.

She walked slowly towards the vehicle, her mind on what she had to do next, before she heard her name called and she looked up. Dougal was walking towards her.

"Dougal? Aren't you working today?"

"No, I'm not. Are you heading home?"

She nodded, then pointed to the vehicle. "With him."

Dougal turned for a moment. "Then, I'll meet you at your place."

"Dougal! Wait! Why?"

"Because we need to talk, Holly."

"Not today, Dougal. Absolutely not today." She turned and walked away from him, leaving him staring after her before he ran to catch up with her, sliding to a stop as John, her security personnel, stepped in between them.

"Holly?" His voice caused her to pause and turn before she walked back towards him.

"What is it, Dougal?" She nodded to John, who stepped backwards, his eyes on Dougal.

"Holly, what is going on? I talked to Doc this morning. He said he had been out to see you and Lincoln last night, that Lincoln had been making plans."

"He was and Lincoln is." She paused, biting at her lip, knowing she should confess to Dougal who had appeared back in her life, but knowing that would put them all at greater risk. "I'm sorry, Dougal. I didn't mean to cut you out. It's just complicated."

"Life is complicated. Your life is way too complicated. Let me help." He knew he was pleading but didn't see he had any choice.

She finally sighed. "All right. Come for supper. Lincoln should be home by then." She reached to hug her lifelong friend.

Dougal nodded and then turned, his mind working. What was she hiding? He knew her well enough to know that she was. Two hours later, he stood in her kitchen, watching Lincoln as he moved around, quiet conversation between the young married couple. He heard footsteps behind him and turned, freezing in place as he stared at the man standing there.

"Dougal? You're all grown up. You're the picture of your father." Callum watched as Dougal's head swivelled between himself and Holly.

Holly moved to stand beside her father, an arm around him. "Dougal? This is why I didn't want you to come. You can't say a word. If you can't do that, then I can't let you leave here."

"Holly?" She could hear the question in his voice.

"It's been too many years, Dougal. You don't remember my father, do you?

He's been around for the last few months. In fact, he's the one who saved me once."

"Your father? Callum?" Dougal swallowed hard. "I didn't know you were still alive. I thought you were dead."

"It's a long story, Dougal, for sharing on another day. Let's just say our not so nice friend, Lyle, decided I needed to stay away and in prison in another country. Doc is the one who found me and got me out."

"Doc?" Dougal shook his head. "He never said a word but then he wouldn't."

"No, he won't. Not unless it was drastic enough for him to do so." Callum pointed to the table. "Let's eat. I've been too many days without enough food to eat."

Dougal watched carefully over the meal, knowing they were not telling him something. He finally sat back, his hand on his mug.

"Holly? What are you planning?"

She shared a look with Lincoln, before she nodded. Callum watched the younger people, seeing the persons they had become and liking what he saw. Thank you, Lord. You have provided just the man my Holly needed. And Dougal has been her brother over the years, someone she has needed.

Lincoln finally spoke. "We need to find Lyle. We know he's been around here. We've seen evidence of that." As Dougal's mouth opened, Lincoln raised a hand. "I know. We should have told you. Told you what? That we found footprints around the property, including in the gardens near the house. That we found evidence of where someone has camped out and watched the house. That we never saw him. Jake has alerted numerous times but we never found him when we searched. Our security guys have been around. He's avoided them. They have never seen him. It's like he's a ghost, wafting in and out."

Dougal's head nodded. "I know what you're saying but you still should have said something."

Holly's hand landed hard on the table, startling the two younger men and bringing a smile of remembrance to Callum, who remembered how his Lizzie would react the same. "Enough, you two! No more of this. From now on, we move forward, looking for him." She shared a long look with her father before she looked over at Lincoln, who nodded, ready to support whatever it was she was about to say. "We're going on the offensive, Dougal. We are going to actively and openly search for him. There will be advertisements in the paper, on television, on the radio, on social media sites, with his picture and that we want to find him to speak with him regarding a personal matter. We're not sitting back any longer. He's destroyed too much of our lives. He's taken a lifetime from both my father and myself. I want this over."

Dougal sat back, shocked at first, and then nodding. This was the Holly he knew so well. She had been different over the last year, but he understood that. Gaining her father back into her life had brought her back to who she was. And he didn't think Lyle fully understood the steel running through her. Few people did.

Lincoln finally rose, clearing off the table, listening as the other three spoke quietly. Holly was not laughing tonight nor smiling much, he noticed. She still looked pale. His hand running across her shoulders, he handed her a pain tablet, but she shook her head, pushing it away, rising instead to reach into the fridge for a ginger ale. She paused, and he could see a thought running across her face.

"Holly?" His voice was quiet enough that only she heard him.

"Lincoln? I'm fine. Just thinking about something." She reached to kiss him and then returned to the table, her focus on her father.

"Holly, are you sure?" Her father's voice held concern.

"I am, Dad. Come tomorrow, Lincoln and I are heading back for that cabin. We're not leaving there until we find him. Don't worry. Don is pulling in extra personnel, he promised."

"I want to be there." Callum was not backing down.

"And so do I." Dougal pointed at her. "You're not going in there without someone from town on your side."

"I know. Both of you will be there, but you have to stay out of sight. It won't work if you are seen. He'll just hide and come after us on another day. We need to end this. It's gone on for far too long."

Lincoln watched late that night as Holly paced their bedroom. He was exhausted but not ready to go to bed. Not while his bride was still up and unsettled.

"Holly? It's more than this. What is it?" He finally rose, stepping into her path and making her stop.

"I don't know, Lincoln. I really don't. I just feel like life is changing on us and I'm not sure how or if we'll survive." She walked into his arms, feeling his love and strength surrounding her. "I just want to go on with our lives and we can't."

"It will be over soon. That much I know."

She nodded. "I know. I just pray we all survive."

Chapter 23

Lincoln stood at the edge of the clearing, his eyes on the cabin, his thoughts muddled as he remembered the last time he saw that building. Logs had been tossed to the side, and the remnants were shattered and broken. There had been no fire, and he wondered at that.

"It didn't burn, Lincoln. Why not?" Holly's words echoed his thoughts.

"Depending on the explosives used, it didn't. Other than that, Holly, I would say God protected you." Callum was angry, seeing once more the cabin. He had tried to get in at times, to get to the two ladies, but had been prevented by the presence of Lyle's men.

Lincoln looked around, seeing Dougal at Callum's side, and knowing that Don had his men surrounding the area. He had talked with Don, laid out their plan, listened as he talked it over and then added and adjusted to what they wanted to do. He appreciated the wisdom and experience Don brought to them.

Callum's quiet prayer caught at his attention and he listened as Callum prayed for wisdom, for protection and for an end to the adventure as he termed it. Callum nodded as he raised his head.

"Let's get this underway. We have no way of knowing if he's here or not."

"I'm sure he is. He's been too aware of where we've been and where we are." Lincoln pulled out his phone and keys and handed them to Dougal. "Holly, let him have yours as well. It's almost as if he's been tracking us."

Dougal froze and then groaned. "We've searched everywhere. How did we miss your phones?"

Holly spun to stare at him. "Our phones?"

"Yeah, your phones. There could be a tracking program on them." Dougal was angry with himself, not having thought of that.

Lincoln reached for Holly's hand, searching her face before he nodded and walked forward, Holly matching his steps. They paused as they reached the cabin.

"It's so horrifying to remember." Holly's face had whitened.

Lincoln's hand tightened on hers. "It was. I thought I had lost you when the cabin came down. When the paramedic's head went down, I was sure. God protected you and Larkin that day." He led her around the debris, his eyes probing. "I have no idea what we're looking for, do you?"

She shrugged. "Not a clue. If it was to lay out a garden, then I would know." She stopped, her eyes on the ground. "Look, Lincoln. Someone has been here. These are fresh footprints."

She looked up at him and then pointed. "They've walked that way. Let's follow them."

"We're not supposed to, you know. We're supposed to stay in the clearing."

She shrugged. "This is not going to solve itself by us staying in the clearing. They can follow us or stay here."

Lincoln gave a small smile. "Your father expected this, you know."

"I know he did. He talked to you too, did he?"

"He did." He walked forward, Holly at his side, as they headed for the edge of the clearing and then through the small strand of trees to stand looking down over an embankment. "There's a path. It looks well used."

"It would be. Now, we'll go down. What will we find?"

He shook his head. "I have no idea, my love."

They finally reached the bottom of the embankment, staring up at the top.

"That's a good fifteen to twenty feet drop." Lincoln was surprised. "It didn't look that far."

"No, it's deceptive. It always has been." She spun in a circle. "We're being watched."

"I know we are. He's here. Pray that today ends it, Holly. We need this over." He paused as he heard a twig snap. "Our guys aren't down here yet, are they?"

"They might be but I don't think they'd have misstepped like that." She slowly turned, stilling as she saw the man standing in the shadows. "And it is not them."

Lincoln had been watching her and turned as well, his eyes on the man. "Is that him?"

"I think so." She stepped backwards.

"Holly, don't move. If you keep moving backwards, he'll know how scared you are."

"Well, I am scared. I'm terrified." She tightened her hold on his hand. "This is it, Lincoln. One of us won't be walking away from here, I doubt about that."

They watched as the man moved towards them, his steps heavy on the grass and dirt, scuffing through them, dust rising in the air behind him. He finally stood in front of them, hands on his hips, a gloating expression on his face.

"I finally have you two right where I want you. In my hands." He shook his head at them. "You tried so hard to escape, but this time, I guarantee you neither of you will walk away." He motioned towards the trees he had come through. "That way. No hesitation, Carmichael, or she dies now."

Lincoln walked forward, Holly behind him, Lyle bringing up the rear. He had pulled out his weapon and had it pointed at Holly's head. She steeled herself not to show her fear, knowing that would feed his ego.

Finally, after about three miles, he told them to stop, brushing by Holly to shove Lincoln forward. Stumbling Lincoln barely kept his balance, turning carefully to watch Lyle and then his eyes went to Holly. She was frowning, her eyes staring past him before she looked at him, a slight nod her only movement. He nodded slightly as well, knowing she had seen something behind him that had given her hope. Who was there, he wasn't sure, but he knew it was a friend. Holly would not have given that signal otherwise.

They listened as Lyle ranted at them, blaming Holly for his having had to leave town when he did, that she had ruined his life, that he had planned the imprisonment of her father as punishment for her.

Holly finally spoke up, her voice bored. "Give it a rest, Lyle. You ruined your own life, you know. You didn't have to sell drugs. You got greedy, wanted money and fame. You're the only one who made that decision. I didn't force you to do anything." She spun to stare at him. "You've affected my life in a way no one man should have been allowed to. You took my father and my mother's husband away from us. Don't tell me we caused that."

He stared at her for a moment before he stormed towards her, the weapon waving in the air, and then spun to storm towards Lincoln, before he stopped, a hand going to his head. Lincoln and Holly shared a puzzled look.

"You're not smart enough to set this up. You were never that smart, Lyle. Who is backing you? Who actually arranged for Dad to be set up?" Holly was pushing for answers.

"I am that smart. I did it all." He turned, anger and hatred contorting his face.

She drew a deep breath, knowing they were at the centre of it now. "No, you're not. You had to have something behind you.

You do the dirty work. He or she makes the plans." Holly's voice trailed off as she said that, realizing they had never considered that a woman might be behind him. Her mind raced as to who it might be, not sure any more of what was truth where he was concerned.

"I am so. I planned it all. No one tells me what to do." He pounded at his chest with one hand, the other waving the weapon around. "Don't tell me you don't believe me. It's the truth."

"I'm sure it's the truth from your standpoint. But I know better. If you were that smart, you would not have given that man the drugs out in the open like that." She backed away a few steps, her path taking her towards the trees she knew was behind her. She knew the men who had come with them were surrounding them. She just needed to get Lyle close enough to the trees and then have him turn his back to them. She just wasn't sure if she would have enough time to do that.

"Your father was weak. He always was. He died in prison, you know." Lyle taunted her, not knowing that Callum had in fact escaped and was in the woods surrounding them, listening to his confession.

Lincoln's eyes raised as he searched the trees. Please, Lord, let someone be taping this. It's his confession. He'll try and deny it but if we have it on tape, then maybe we can use it against him.

Lyle spun suddenly, moving towards Lincoln, his weapon raised to hit at him. Lincoln's arm went up but he was just not quick enough. The blow took him to the ground, where he lay, a hand on his face where the blow landed, Holly's screams echoing in his ears. He didn't see Holly launch herself at Lyle's back, her fingers reaching to scratch at his face and eyes. He barely heard the shout of pain and anger that Lyle gave and didn't see him fling Holly away from him. Holly landed awkwardly, her head hitting and sending pain through it, before she was hauled to her feet and the weapon planted firmly against her temple.

"That's not what you want to do, girl. That will get you killed too quickly." The weapon moved and pointed at Lincoln. "First, we'll kill him and then you. Or will we wait until he's on his feet again and kill you and let him watch?"

Holly began to feel terror rising within her and her heart cried out to God for protection. Her vision narrowed to the point all she could see was Lyle. She didn't hear the sounds of running footsteps, of calls for Lyle to put down his weapon. She didn't feel him swing around, her body limp in his clutches, as he spun to face the men approaching him.

Lyle paled as he saw the older man. "You! You're dead! They told me you were killed!" His hand began to shake and Holly slid from his grasp as it loosened, to land in a limp heap near him.

"No, Lyle. I'm not dead. You tried hard, but it didn't work." Callum shook his head in pity. "You've ruined how many lives now? You always were greedy and grasping, wanting what others had and not willing to work for that."

Dougal's cuffs snapped around Lyle's wrists with a sharp click and he pulled him away, heading for the patrol vehicle that was waiting. Two of Don's men's headed out with him.

Holly crawled the space that separated her from Lincoln, her hand on his face, calming him as only her touch could. Callum crouched beside her, a frown on his face as he saw Lincoln relax under Holly's touch.

Lincoln roused, his eyes on his wife. "Holly, are you okay?"

She nodded, the pain from her headache radiating through her. "And you? He hit you hard, my dearest."

Lincoln sat up, Callum's hands reaching out to help. "He did. I couldn't get myself together to get to you." He looked around. "Where is he?"

"Dougal's arrested him and taken him away." Callum sat on the ground, his eyes on his daughter. "It's over, Holly. All over."

She nodded as she hugged him and then turned to Lincoln, finding refuge in his arms. "Is it, Dad? I don't think so. There has to be someone behind him."

"That's something the authorities will look into. They will find them."

Holly shivered, cold fingers reaching around her spine. "I hope so, Dad." She looked up at Lincoln. "Lincoln?"

"Yes, my dearest?" He hugged her tight. "Let's get you home."

Don appeared just then, his voice startling them. "First, we get you checked out and then you can go home."

Chapter 24

A month later, Holly dug out the envelope Doc had given her. She knew it was time but she still wasn't sure she should open it. She felt Lincoln's hand on her shoulder before she was scooped up into his arms and then carried to their favourite chair in the living room. She cuddled close, her arm around his neck, her hand on his face.

Lincoln watched her closely, seeing how rested she had become but seeing something he didn't recognize in her face. What is it, Lord? What is she going through now?

"Dougal called." His voice was quiet.

"He did? When?"

"About an hour ago. I had to think through what he said." Lincoln paused, knowing his next words might not be taken well. " Lyle admitted all those photos, carvings, calls, foot prints, the papers with his plans for you were his work and his alone. He hired the men to follow us, to track us, and to terrorize us. He finally admitted he was working for someone, had been all his life. He has refused to name that person."

"I didn't think he'd say. That's not his character." She watched him closely. "What else?"

"There will be no trial. God has become his judge and jury. He died from a brain aneurysm early this morning."

She sighed. "I'm glad. I didn't want to go through a trial." She laid her head on his shoulder, her eyes on the envelope. "Now we can go on with your lives."

"That we can. Your father is moving into a house in town. Doc's been helping him reacclimatize to here. Hank's hired him to work in the store."

"That's good. That's what he needs." She stopped, her voice dying away. "I can never get back those years we lost, but God has been good. He brought Dad back to us, He kept us safe through everything."

"That he has." Lincoln reached to kiss her. "Now, that envelope? Will we ever open it?"

She nodded. "We will. Just to clarify, we solved everything for us right? All the threats, assaults, what have you?"

"We did. And that picture of your Mom. That was your Dad who placed it. He was trying to let you know he was around."

"I wondered. Larkin is doing okay? I haven't talked to her in about a week?"

"She has her moments, but she says she's getting there." He tapped the envelope. "Putting it off doesn't change the contents."

She sighed, then reached to loosen the flap. "I know. I just know this will be life changing for us." She pulled out a photo, a frown on her face. "What on earth? What has Doc done?"

Lincoln reached to study it, a frown on his face that changed to a huge smile. "Holly, do you have any idea what this is?"

"Yeah. A black photo with white and gray squiggles on it." Her voice died away as the realization of what it was sunk in. "Lincoln? Is that what I think it is?"

"An ultrasound picture." He reached to turn it over, seeing handwriting on it. "Doc! Of course he would take this way of telling you, not wanting to worry you."

She read the penned words. "Holly, Lincoln, congratulations are in order. You two will make great parents. Come see me when you've finally opened the envelope. I know you too well, Holly. You'll delay opening this for as long as you can. God bless you both and your new little one."

She buried her head against Lincoln, tears near the surface. "No wonder I've felt like I have. I thought it was just what I had been through."

"No, it was more. God has been good." He sat for a moment. "Wow! I was not thinking this."

"Nor was I. Lincoln, God has certainly been working in our lives. I never thought when I found you that day we'd marry, go through all this, and then find we're going to have a baby."

"I certainly didn't either." His head bowed and he prayed, asking for God to provide what they needed and to lead them to trust Him more and more.

Jake chose that moment to stand up at them, nosing at the ultrasound before he gave it a lick and then reached to lick at Holly's face and then Lincoln's. Holly gave a giggle, stating that Jake approved.

Lincoln just held her, content, knowing that he was where he needed and wanted to be. God had led His pilgrim to his home and hearth.

Dear Readers

Thank you for choosing to read *His Pilgrim*. It was not what I envisioned when I put fingers to the keyboard but like always the characters have driven the story and taken it where they wanted it. All I could do was go along for the ride.

We truly are pilgrims here on earth. Heaven is our home and our journey, no matter how long or how short, leads us there. God has provided a home for us there. With loved ones gone ahead, there are days we truly do wish to be there.

Evil is becoming more rampant every day that dawns. Violence has become a way of life. There are just too many stories of bombings, shootings, wars, etc, every day in the news. Drugs are becoming more and more prevalent with dangerous drugs taking more and more lives. That has become a sad fact of life for many.

We are called to witness, to share our faith. It can be done in many ways, other than the spoken word. Let us choose each day to do that. Let us choose each day to look for the God moments, those little things He sends our way.

During the writing of this, I had to let one of my cats go. She was too sick and I couldn't let her suffer. It is always difficult to face those kinds of duties, but God is with us through them all, holding us in His arms to bring comfort and peace just like He provided comfort and peace for Holly all of her life. His plans are so much greater than ours, but He doesn't expect us to know them, only follow Him, to be the pilgrim witness He wants and asks us to be.

God bless each one of you.

Ronna